I CAN'T SLEEP

Philippe Dupasquier

WALKER BOOKS
LONDON

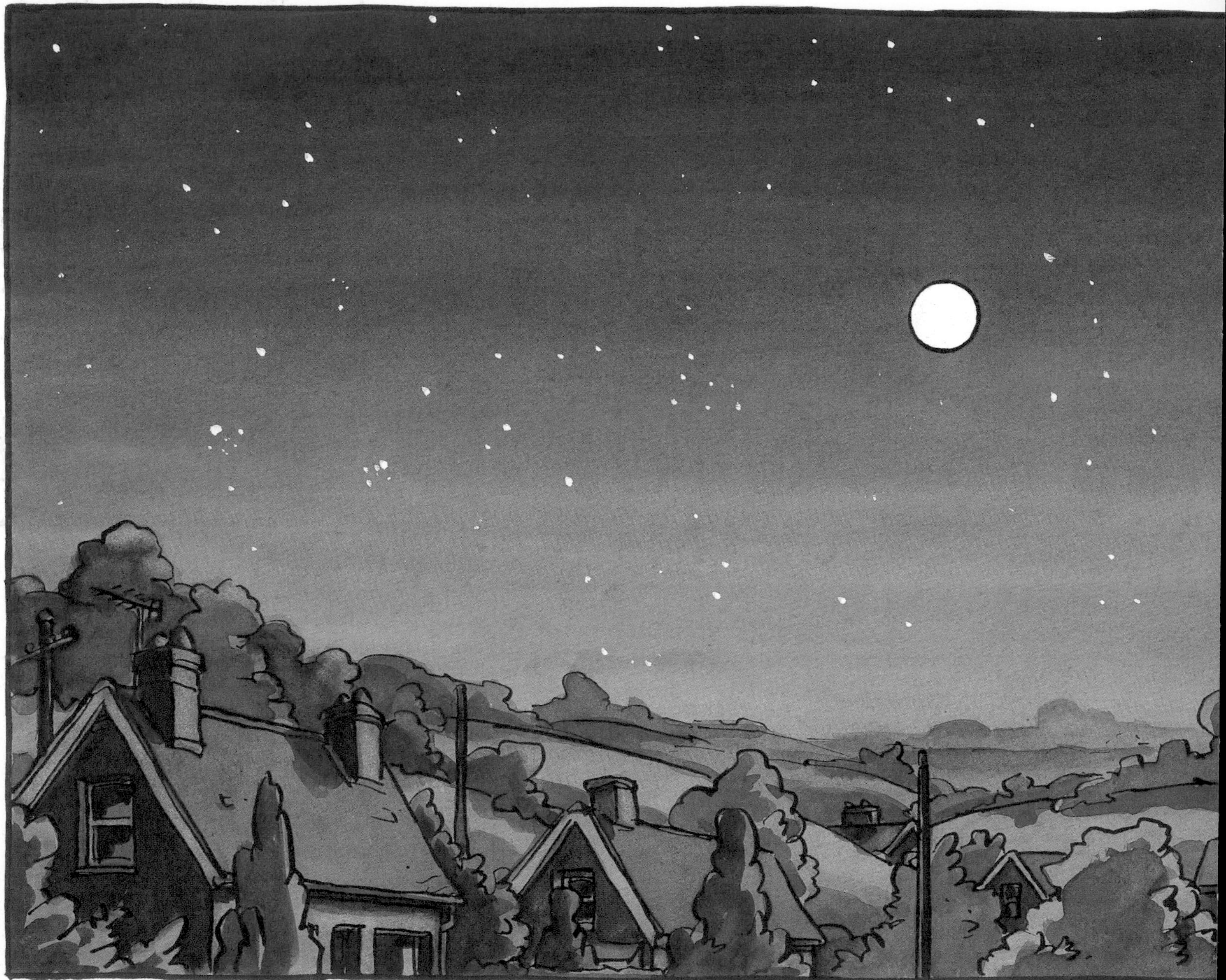

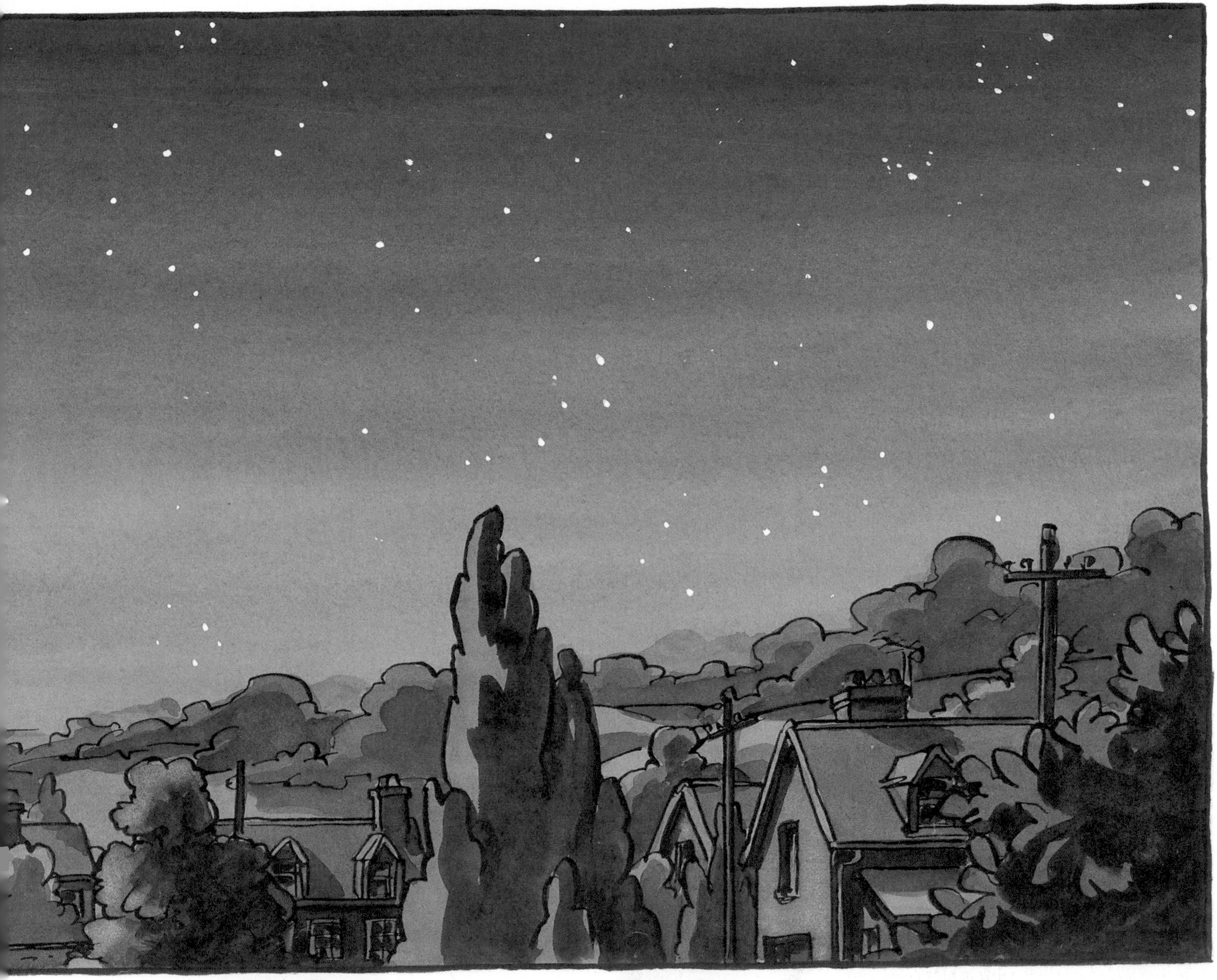

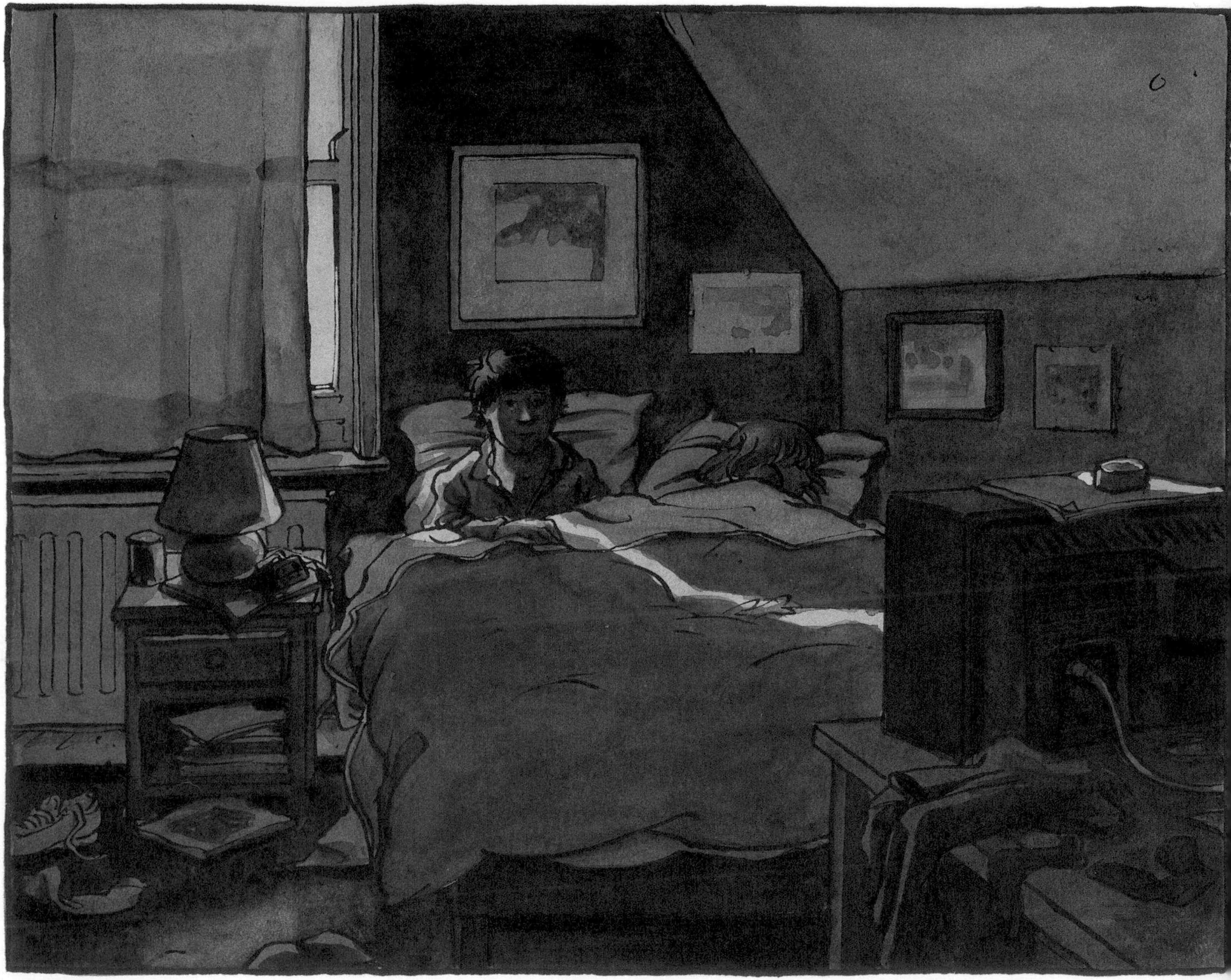

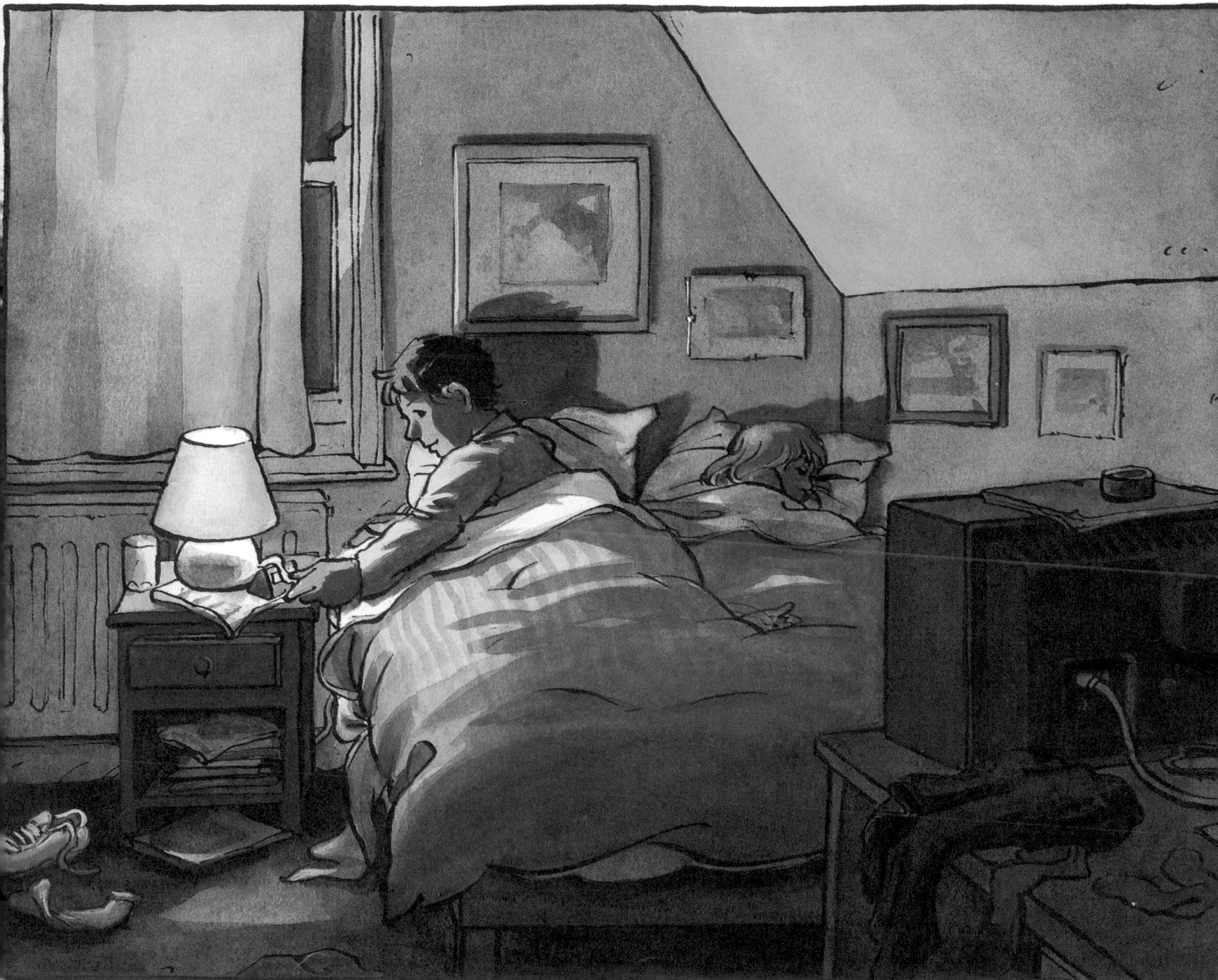

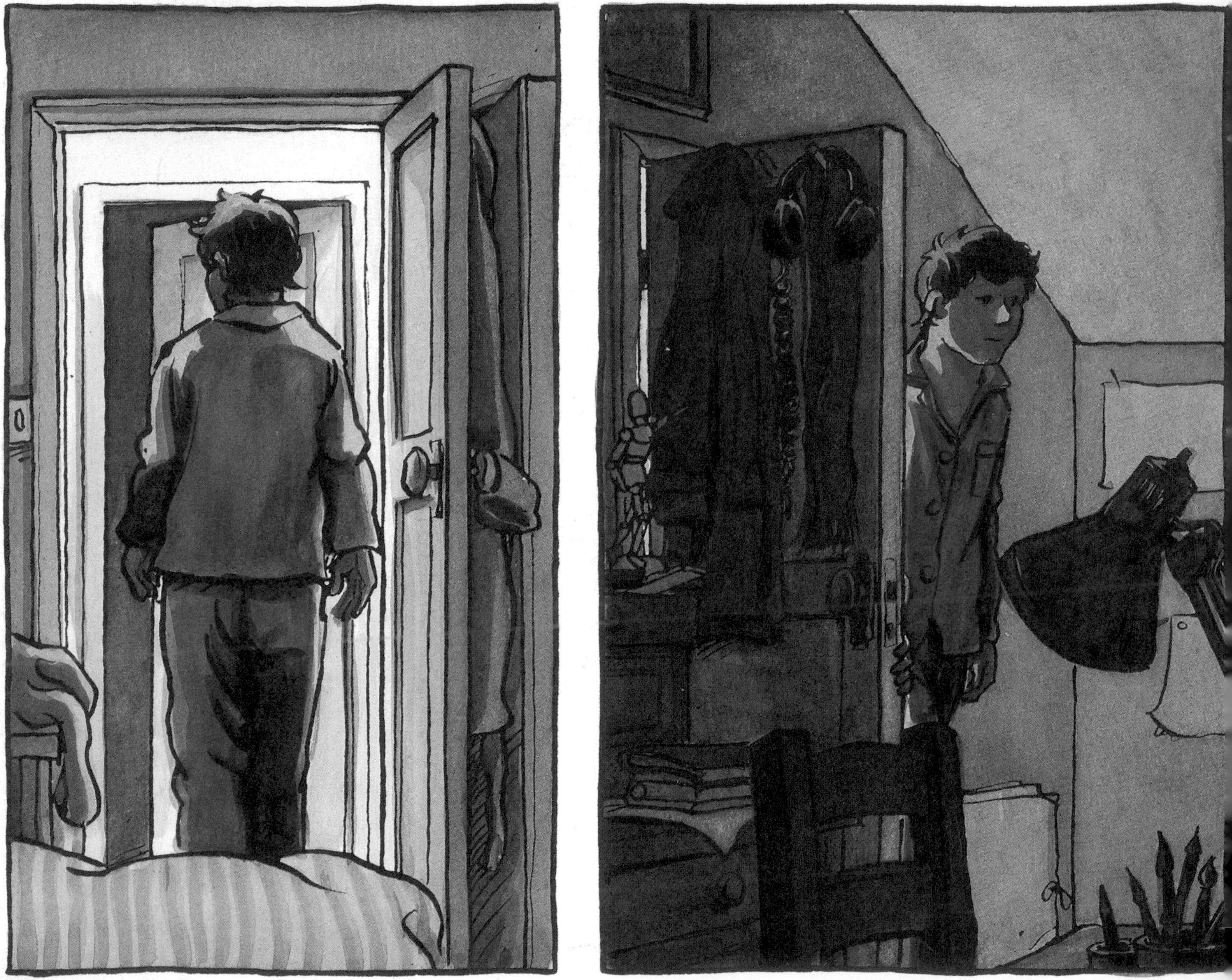

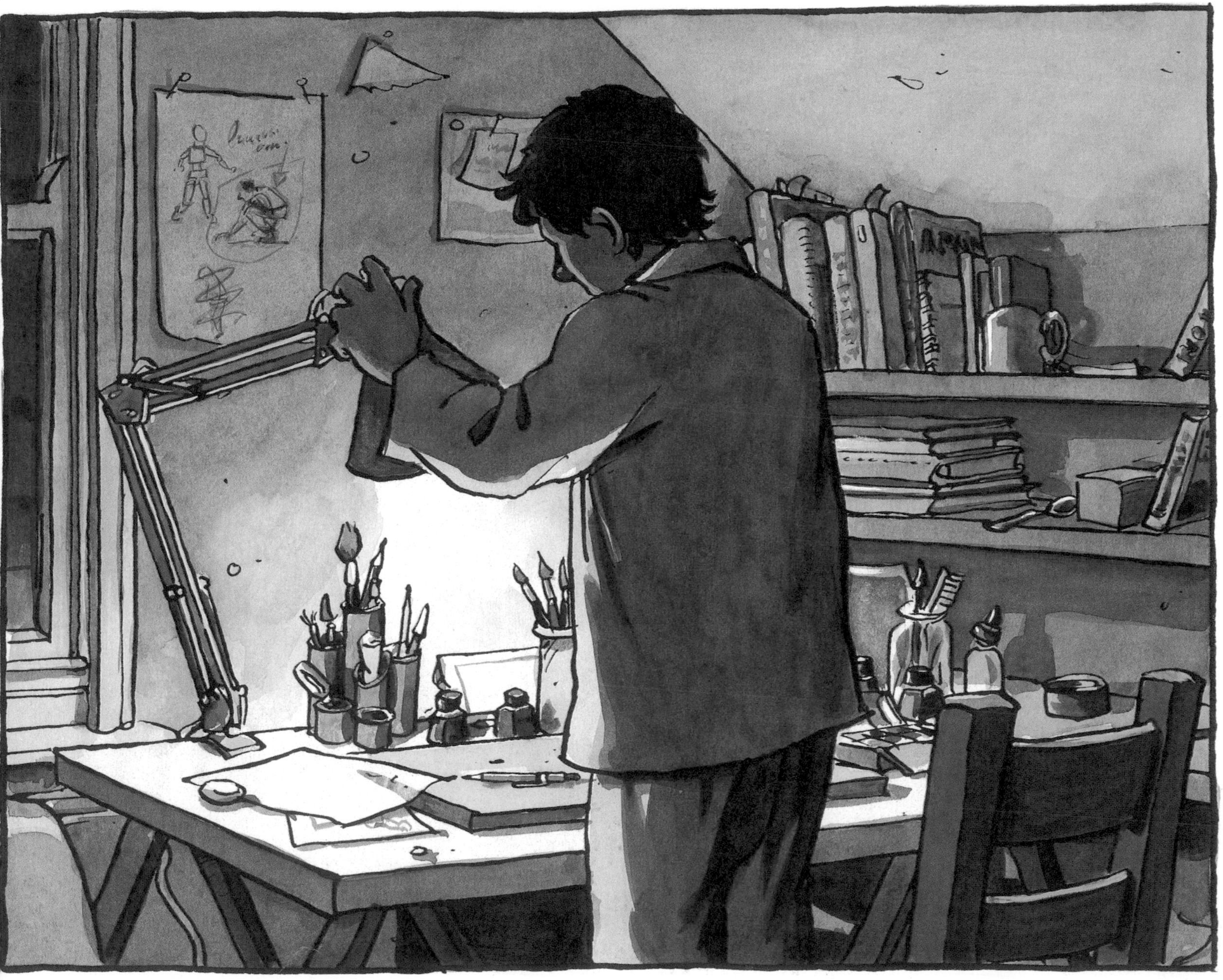

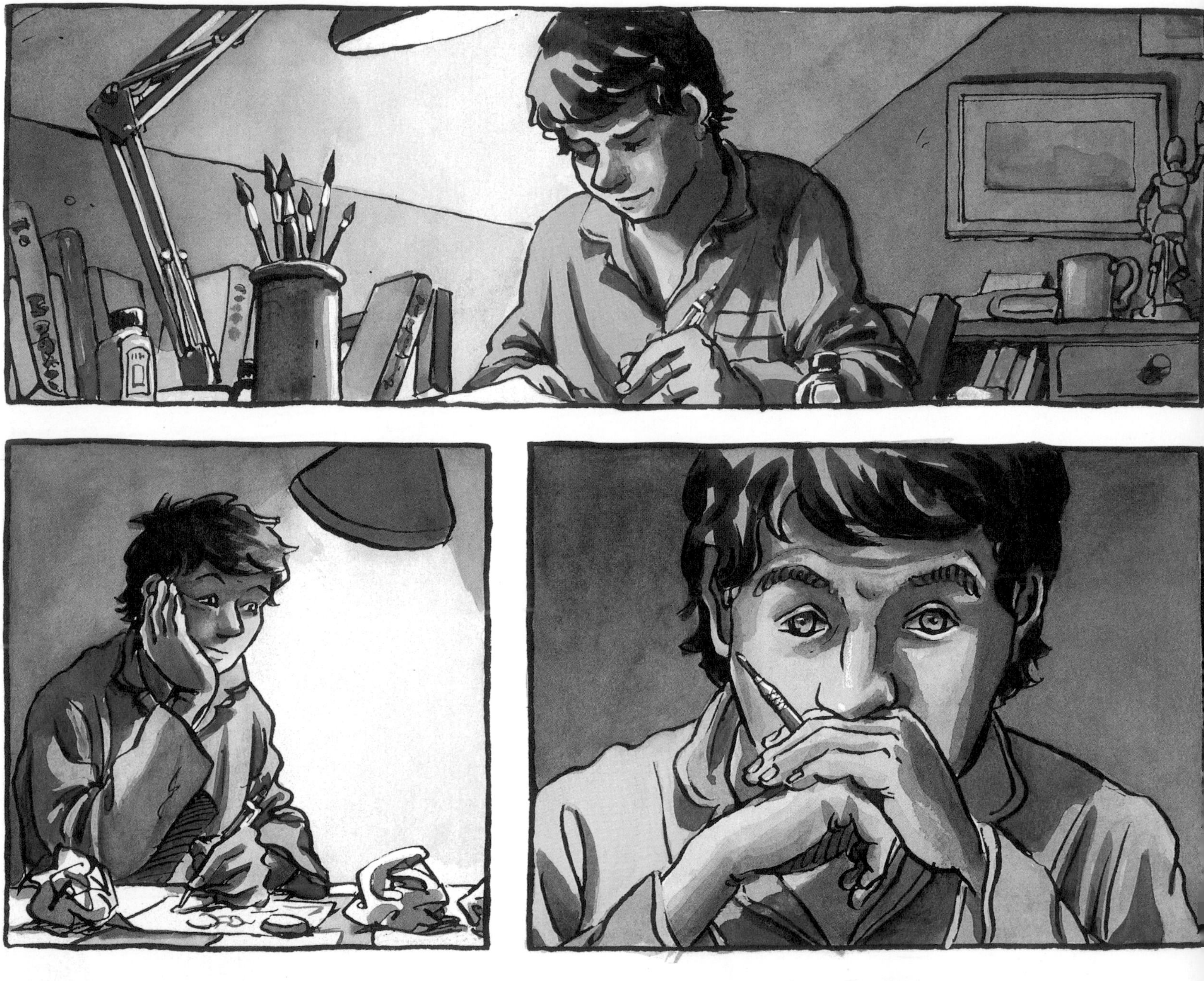

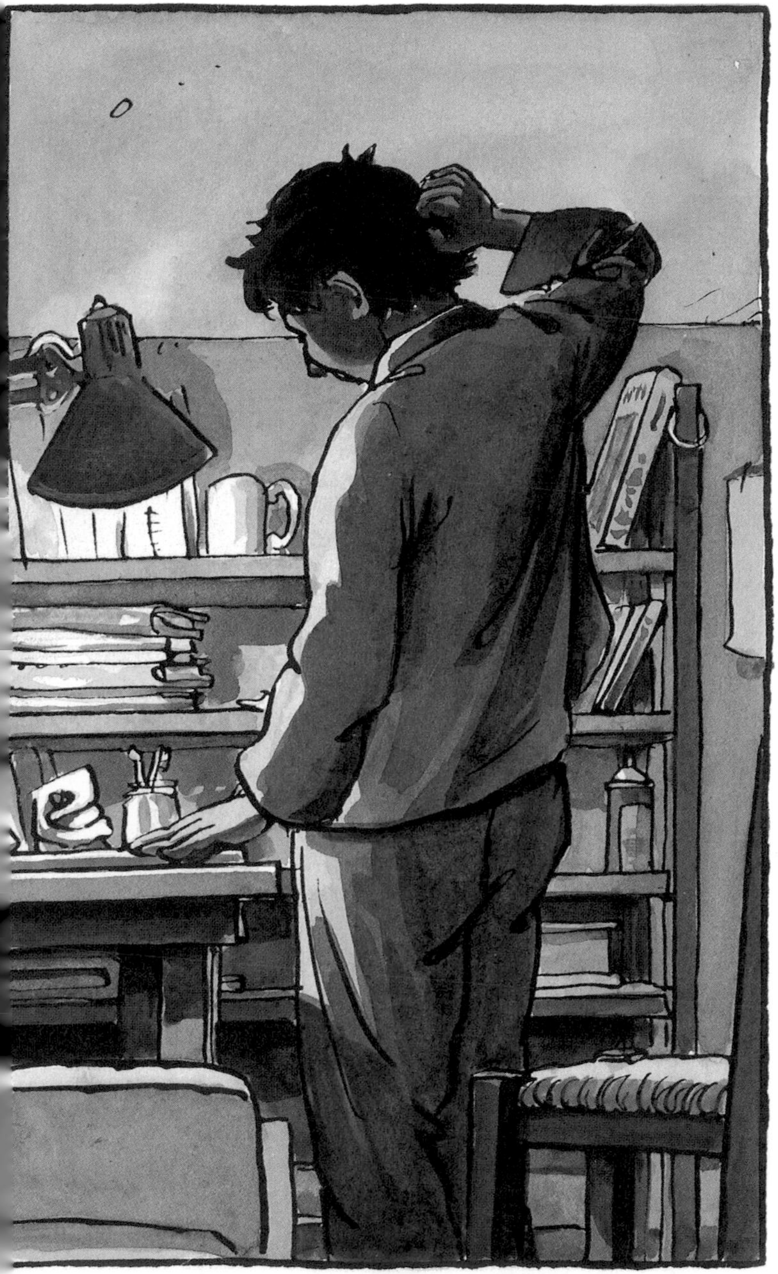
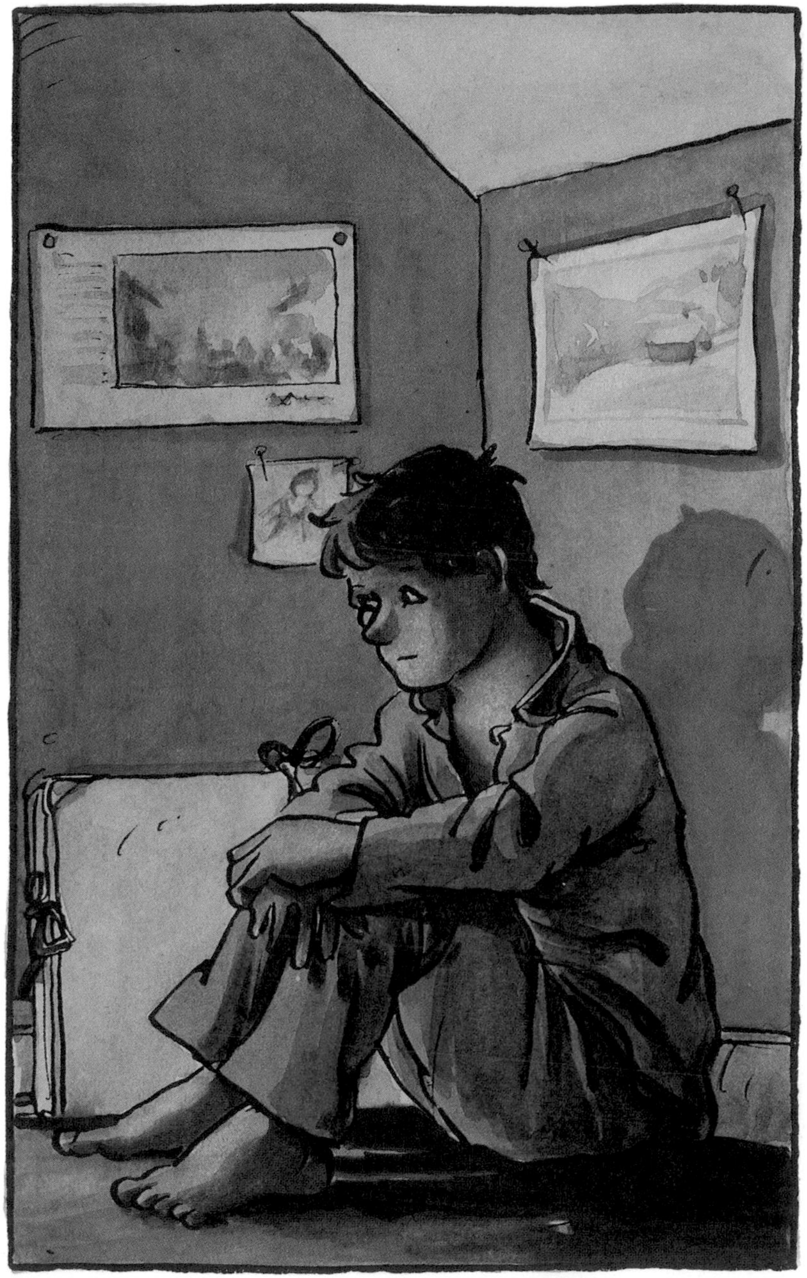

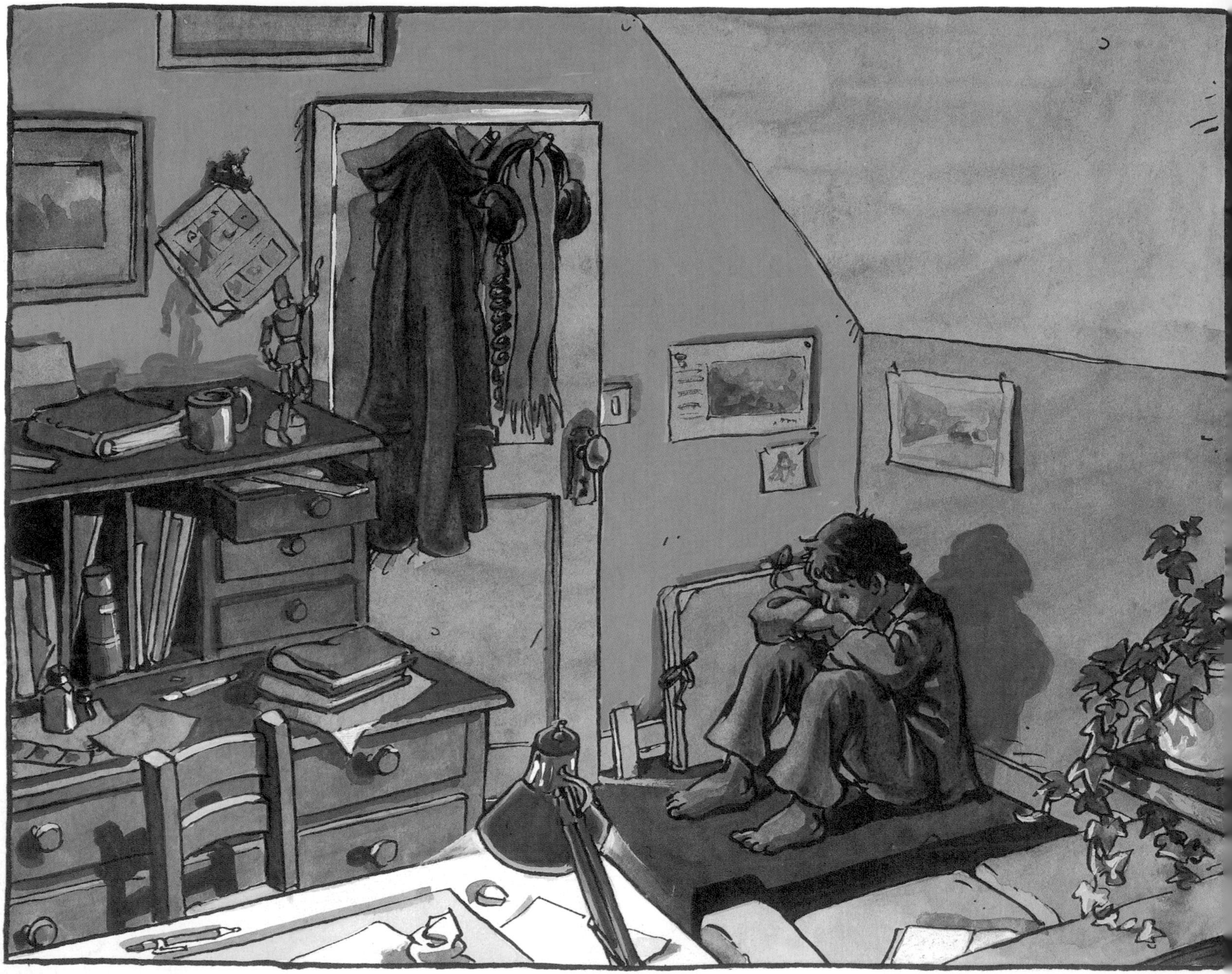

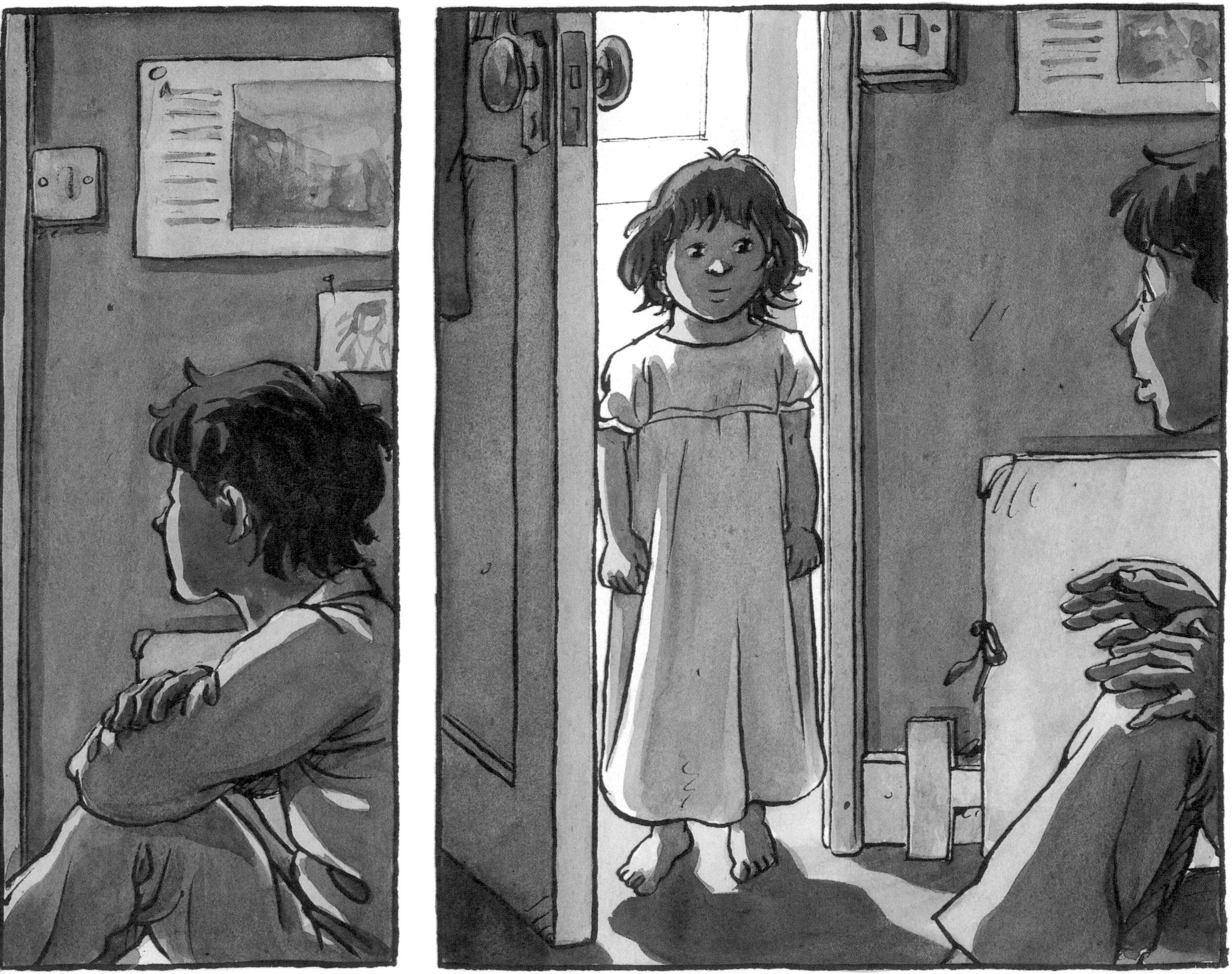

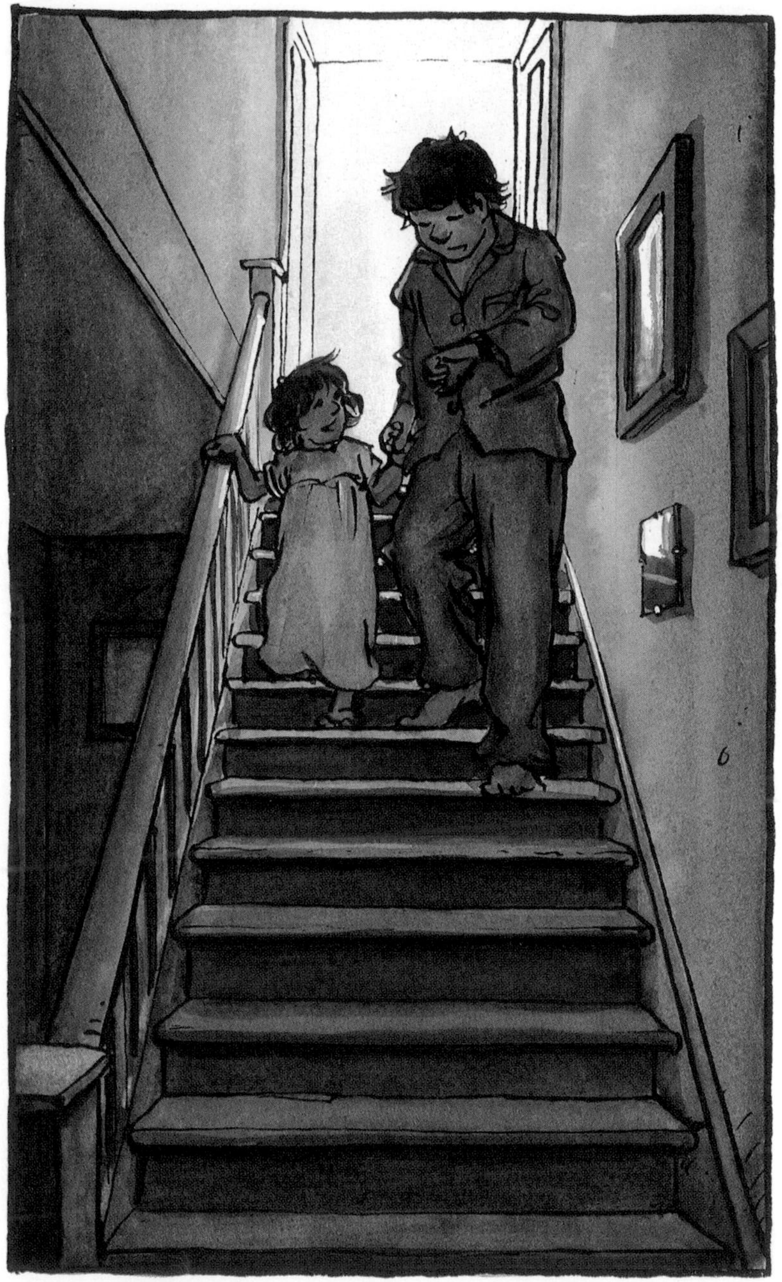
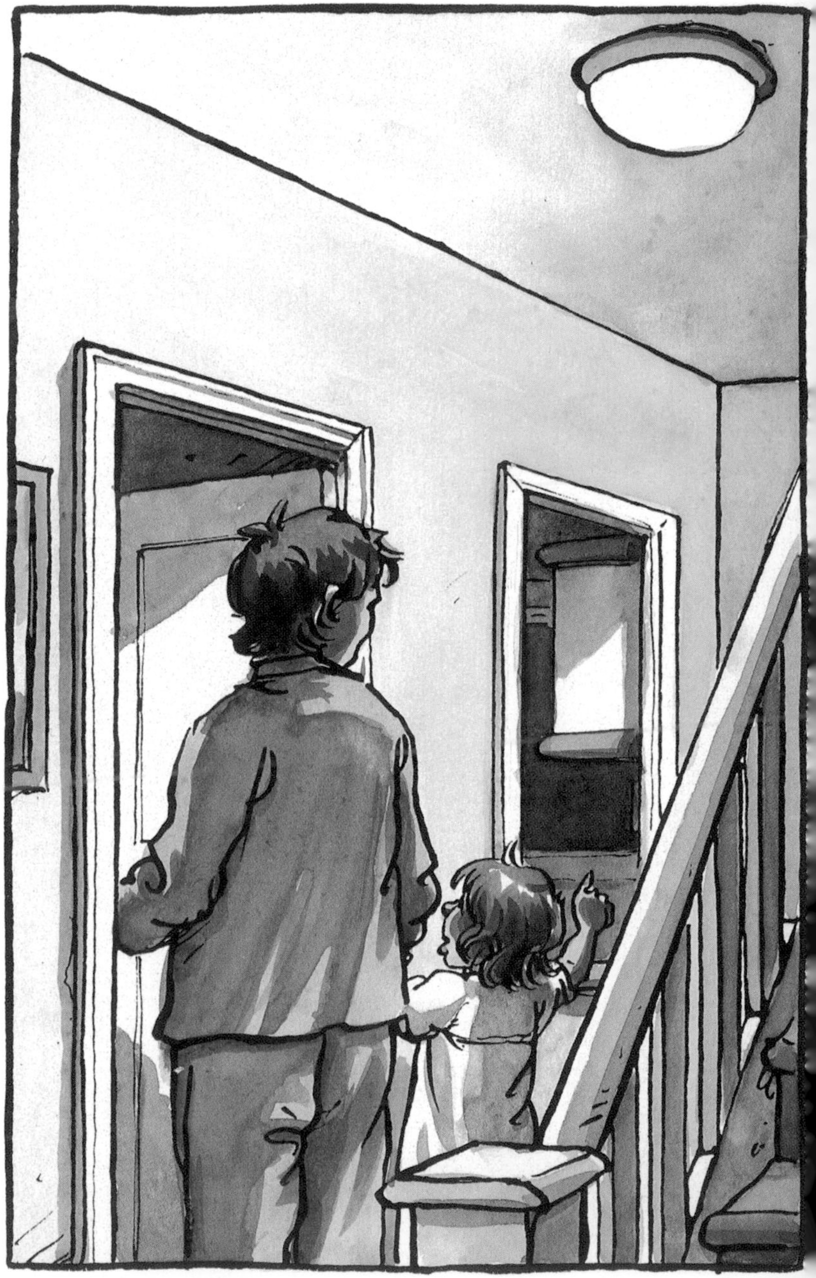

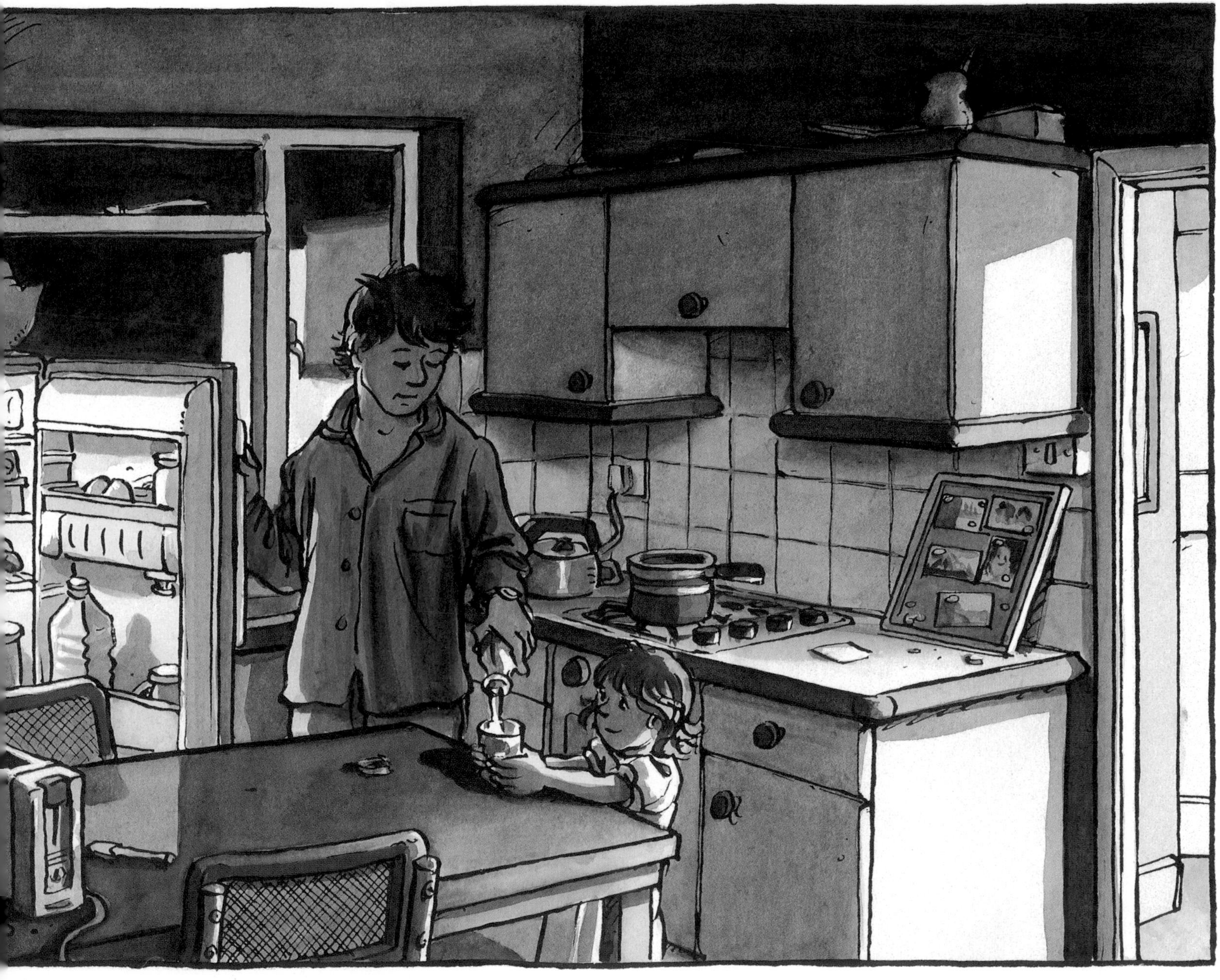

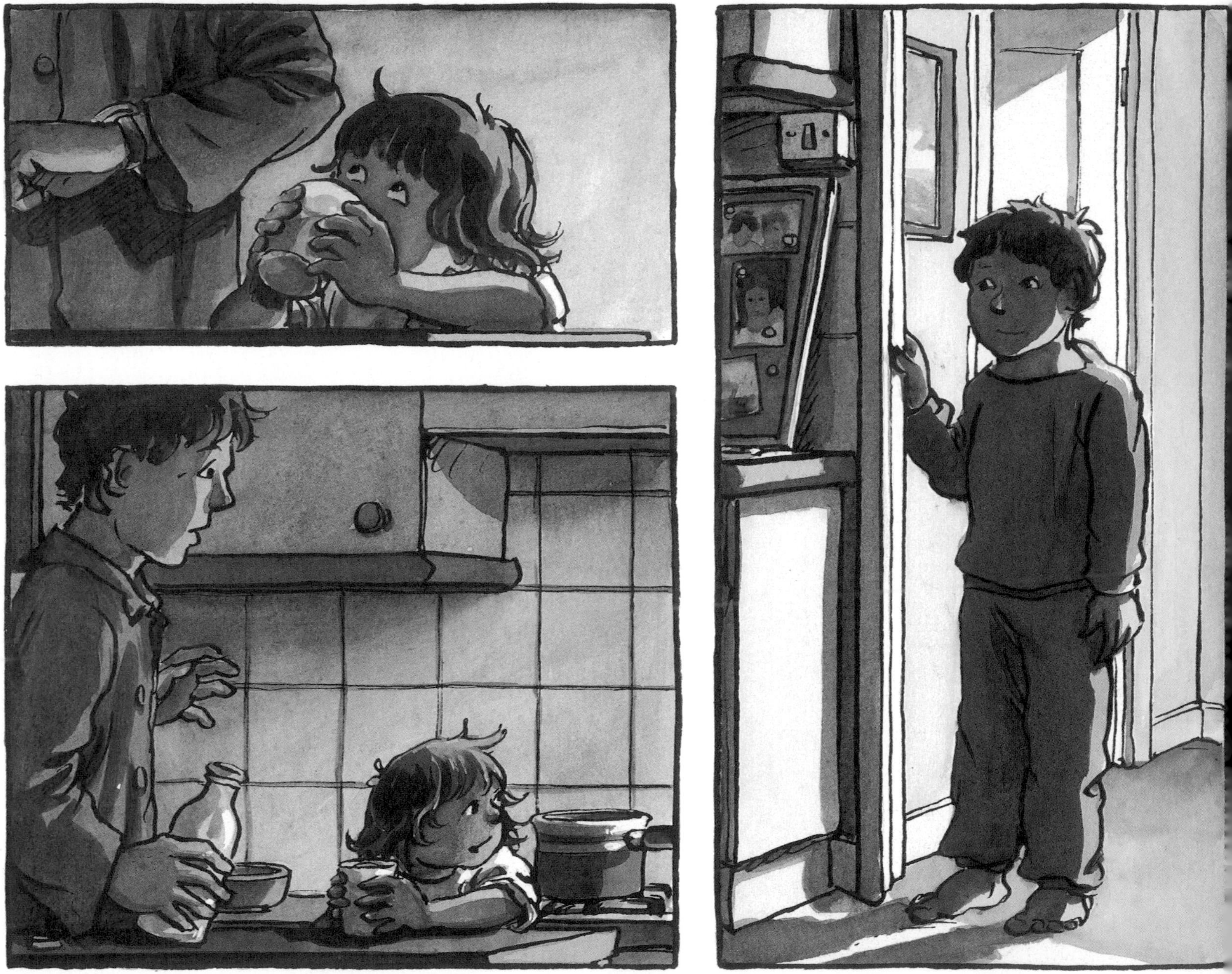

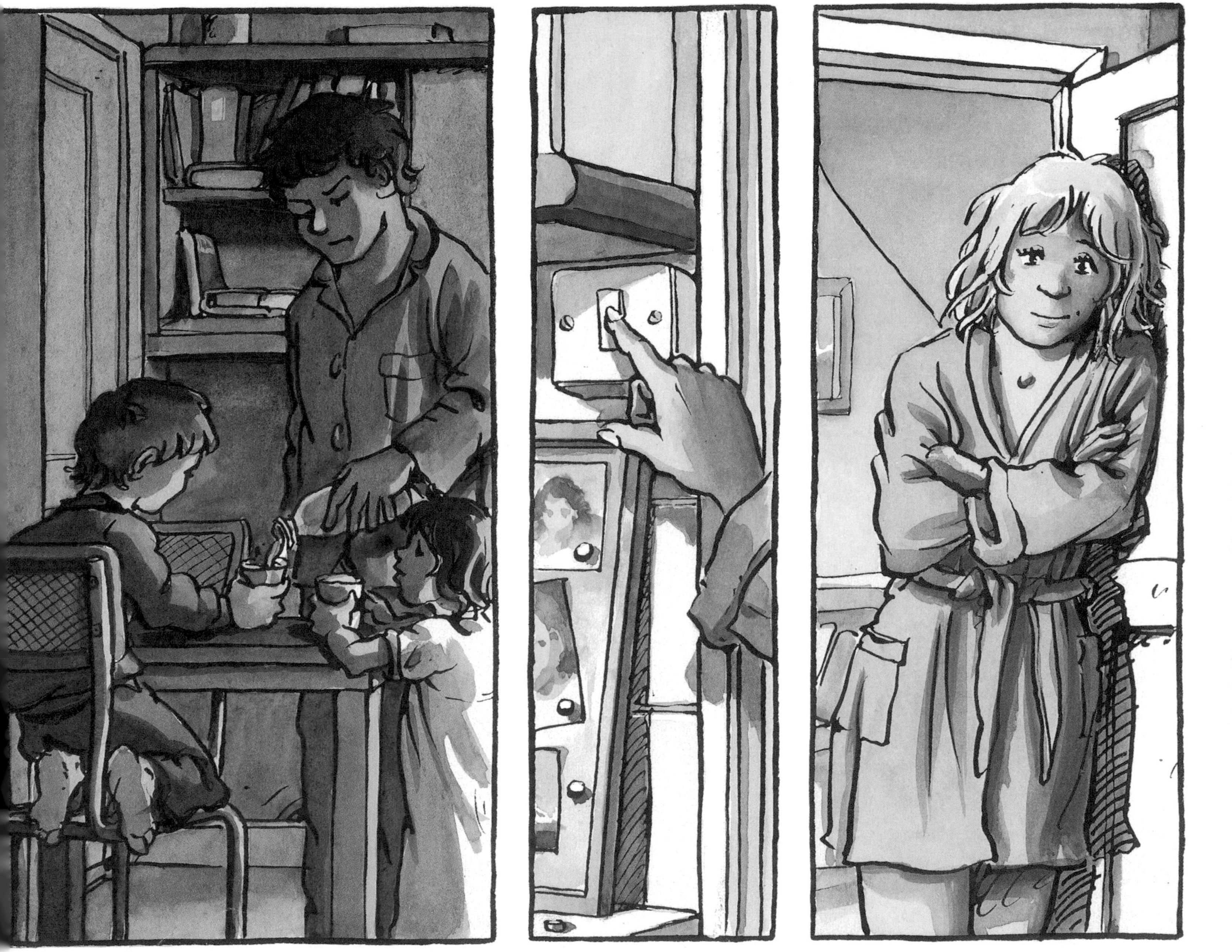

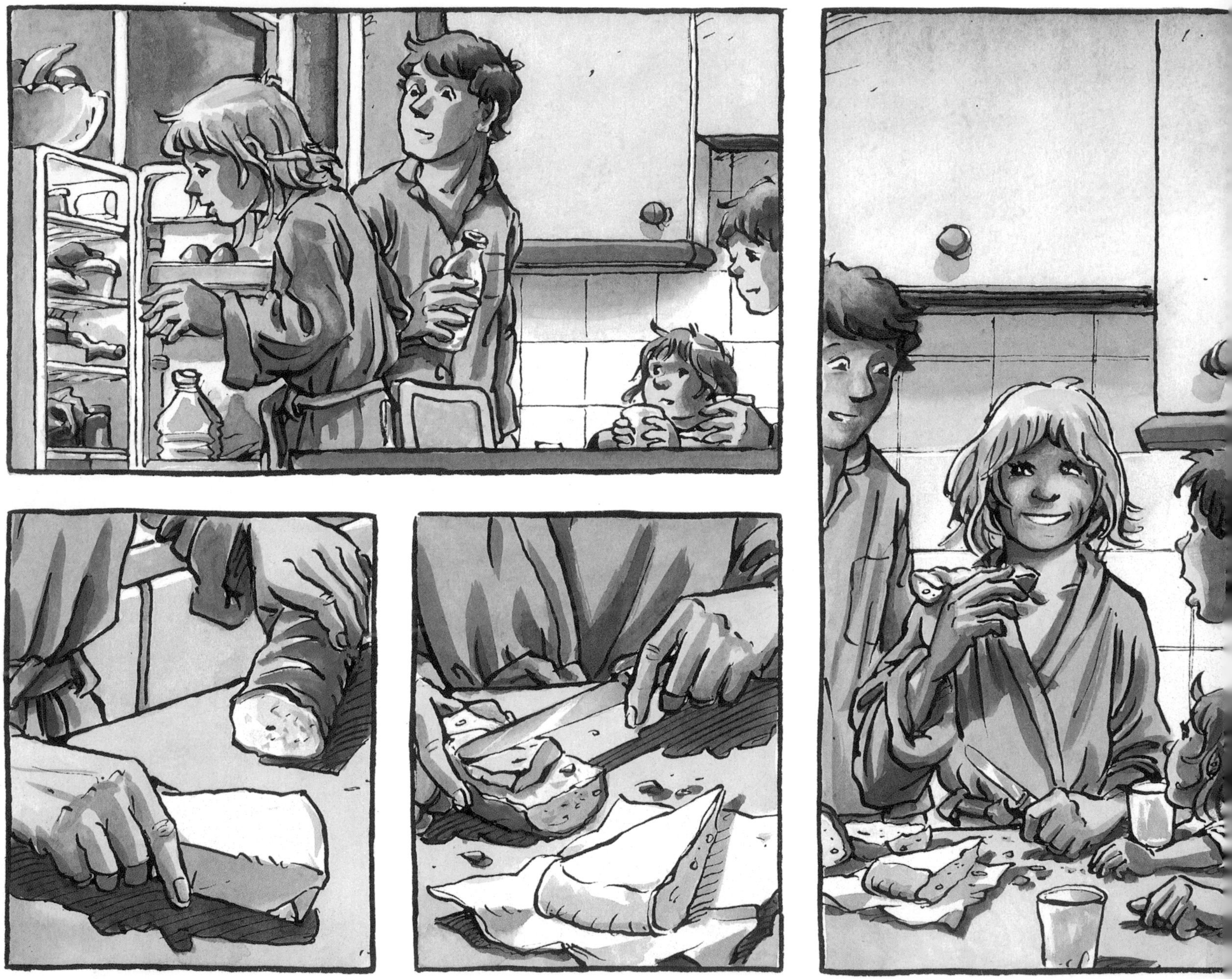

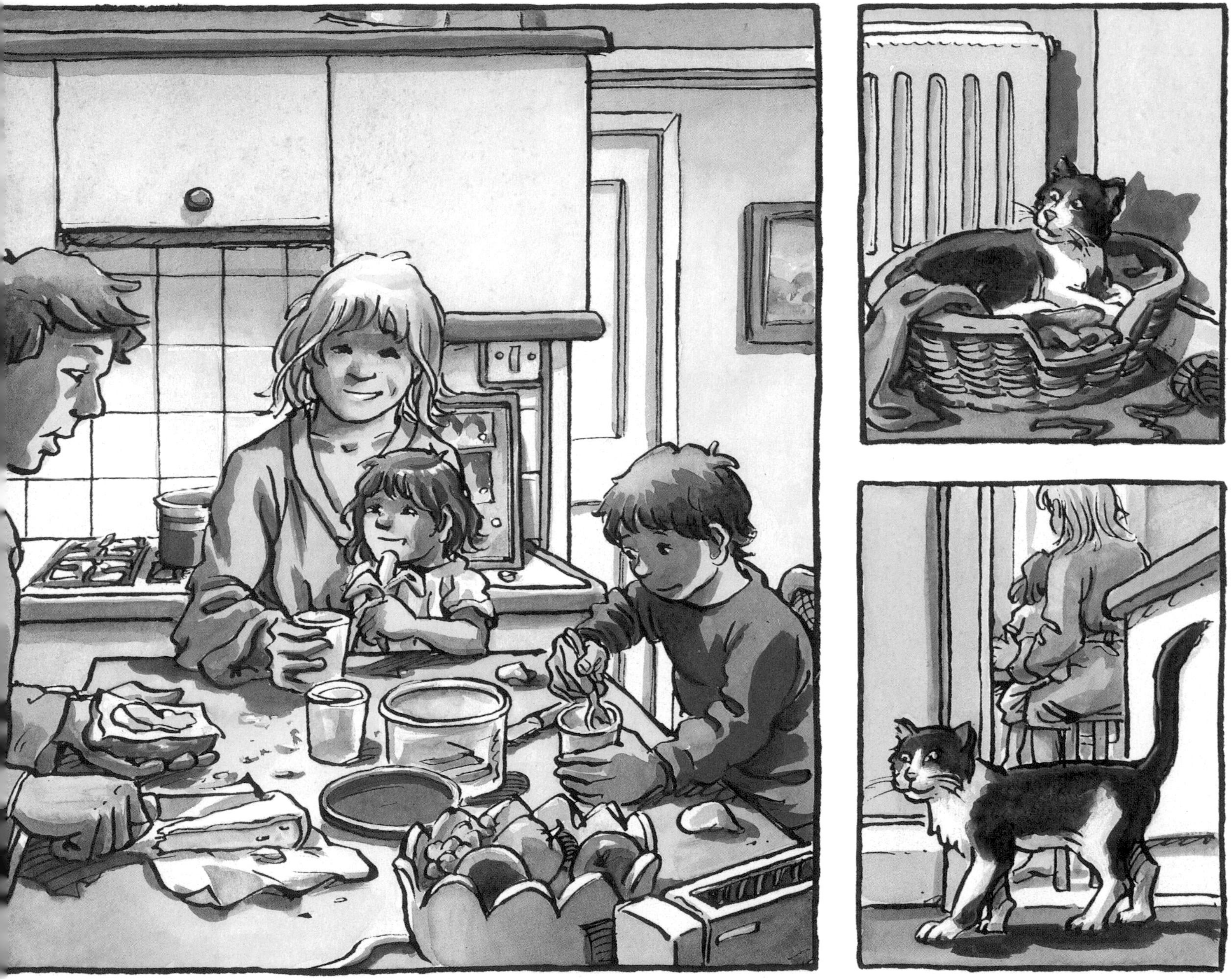

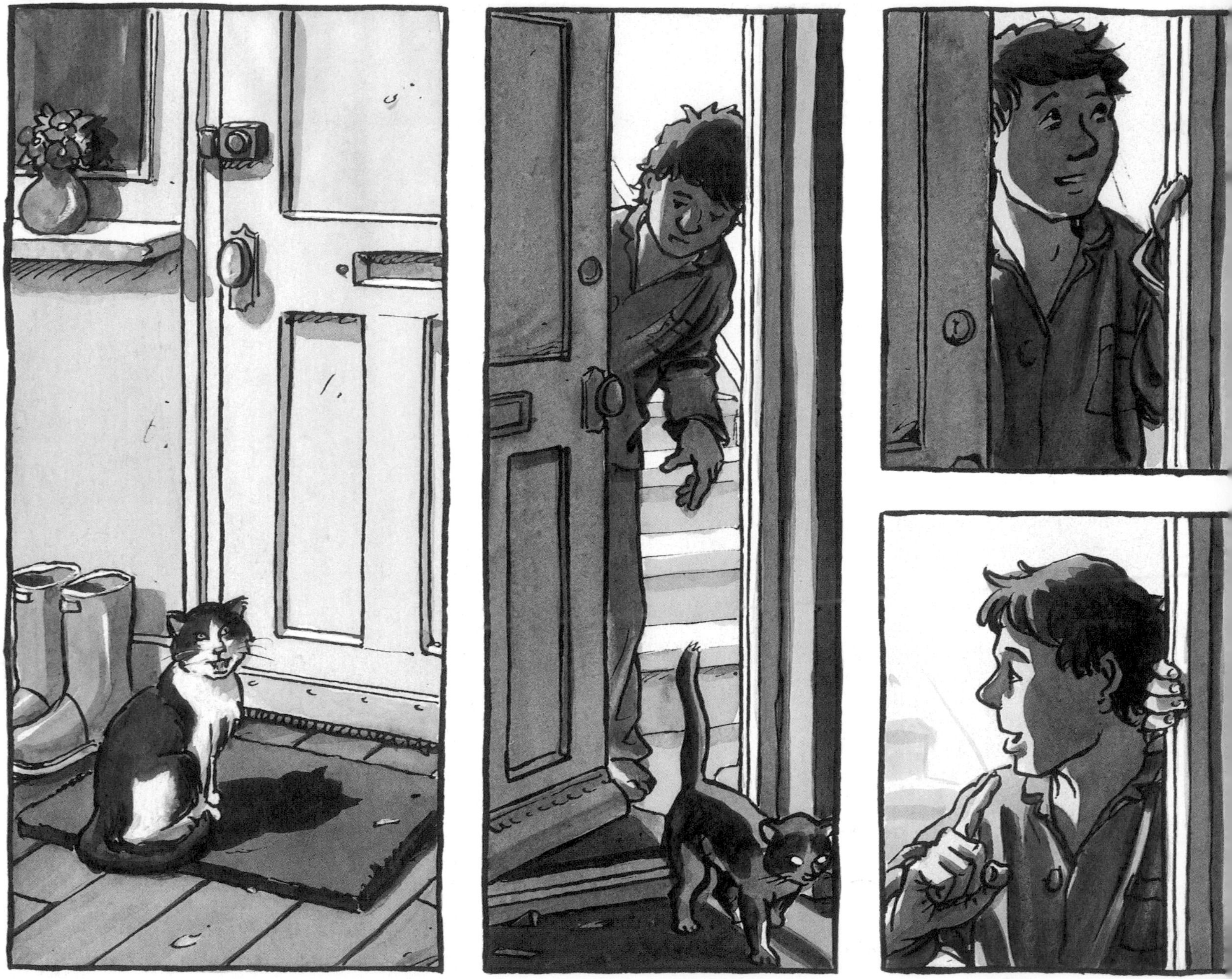

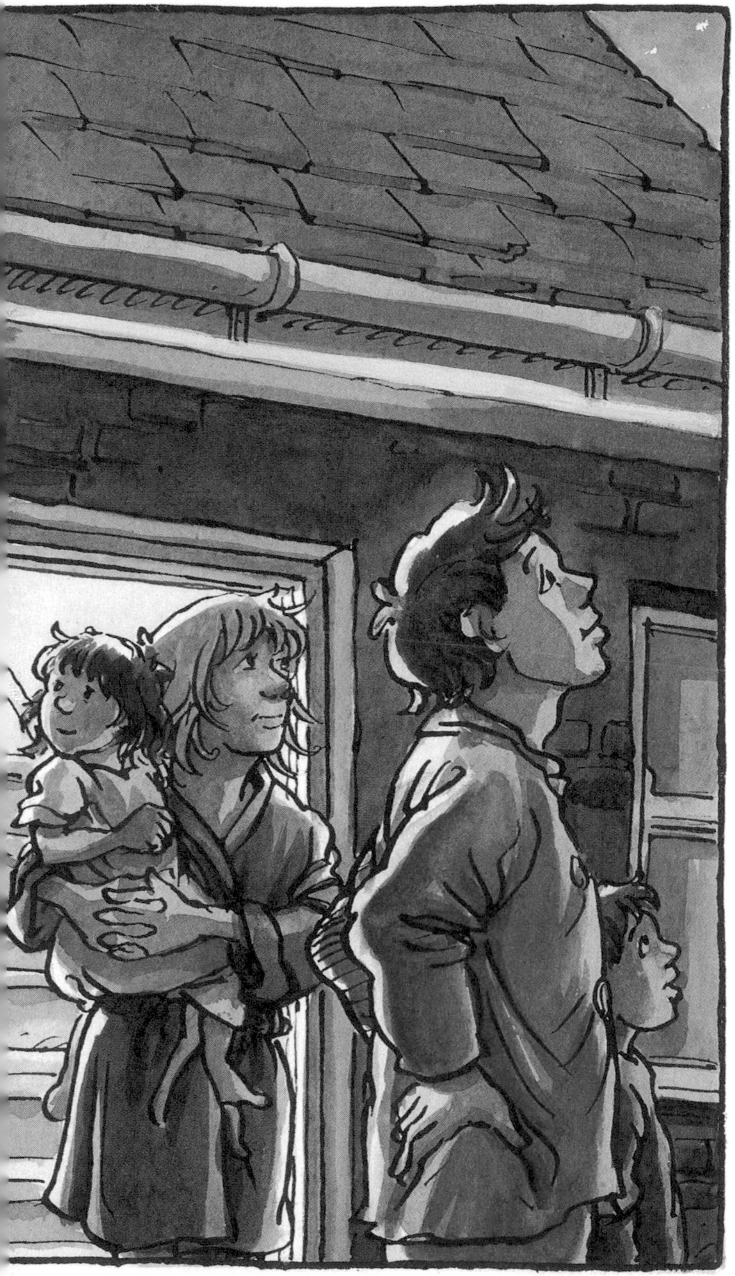
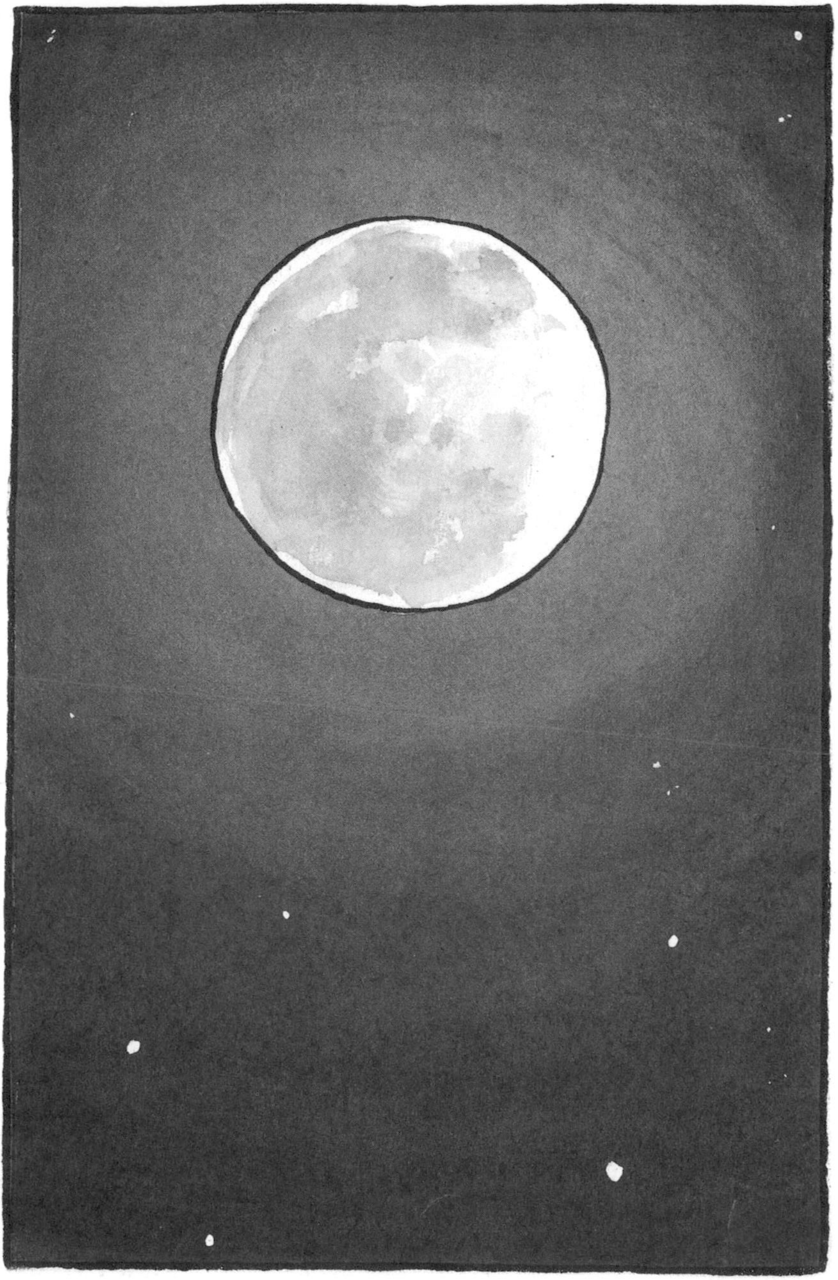

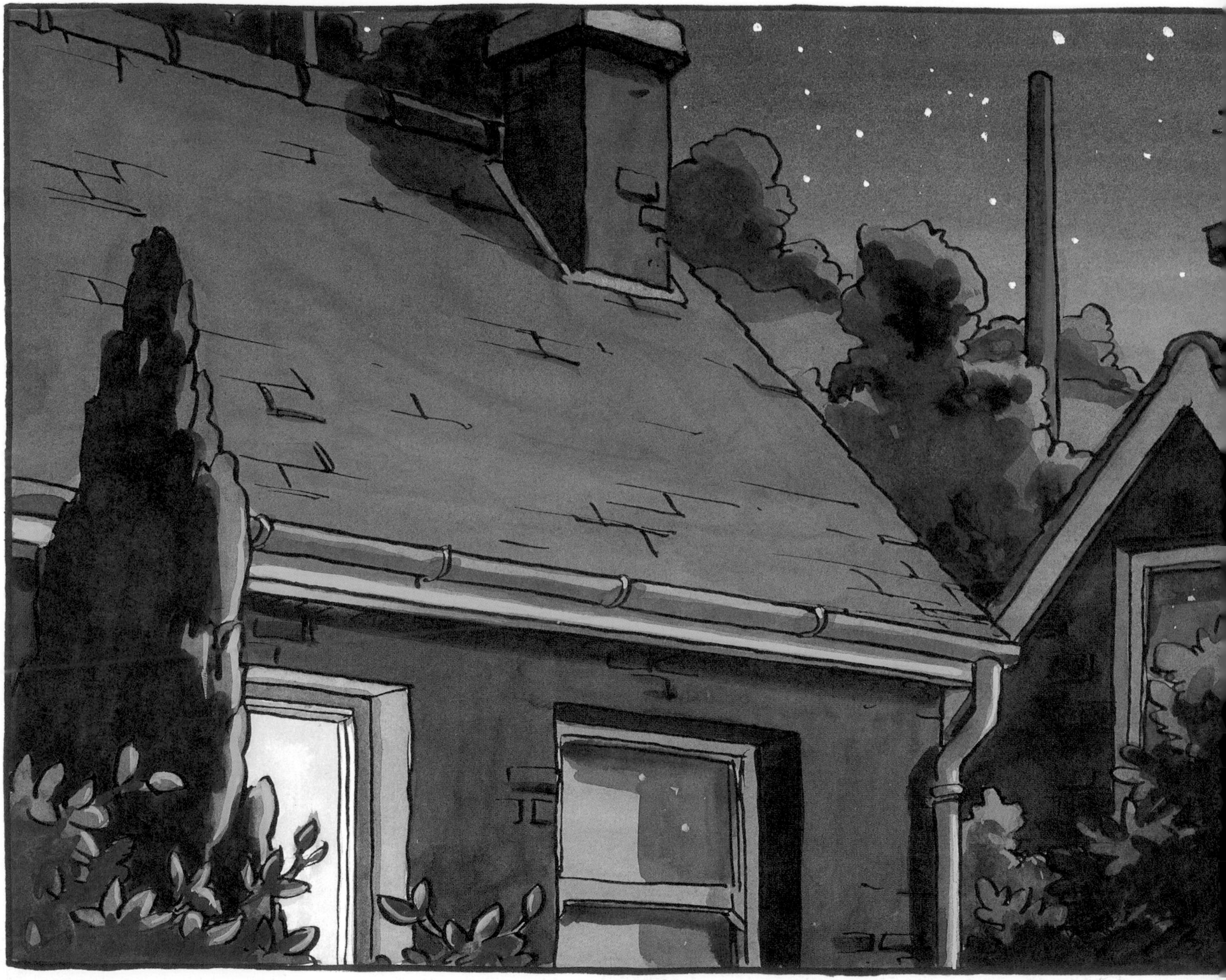

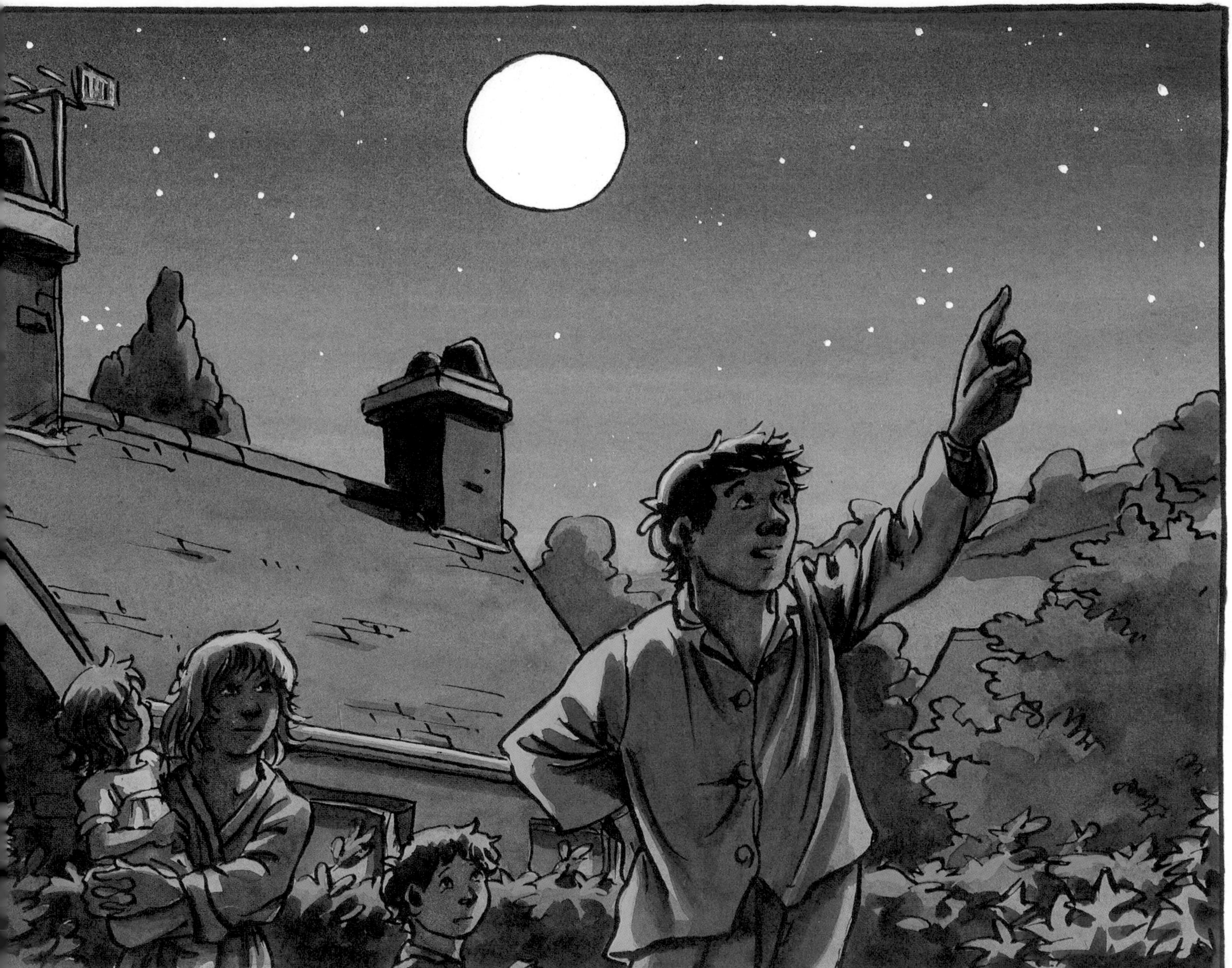

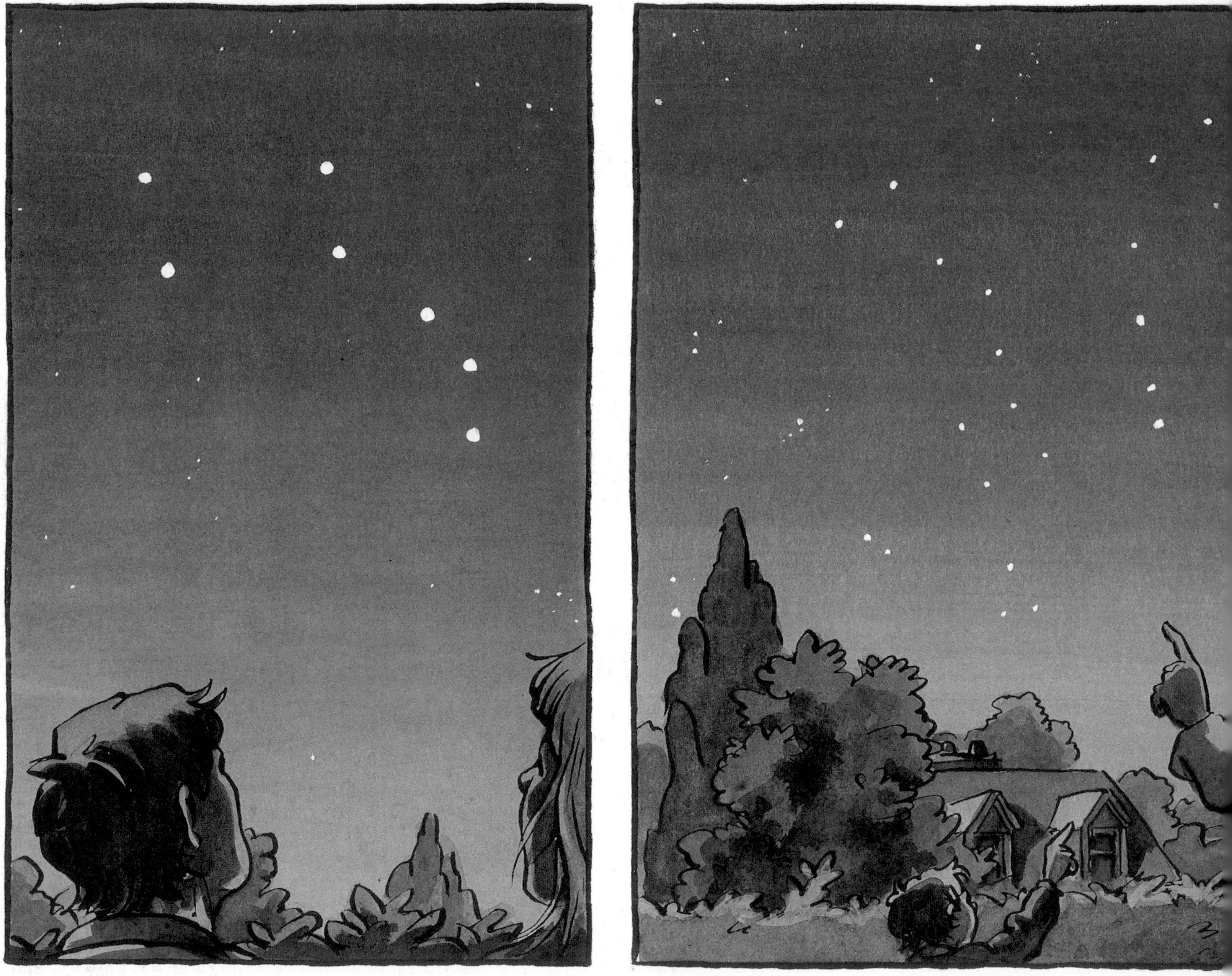

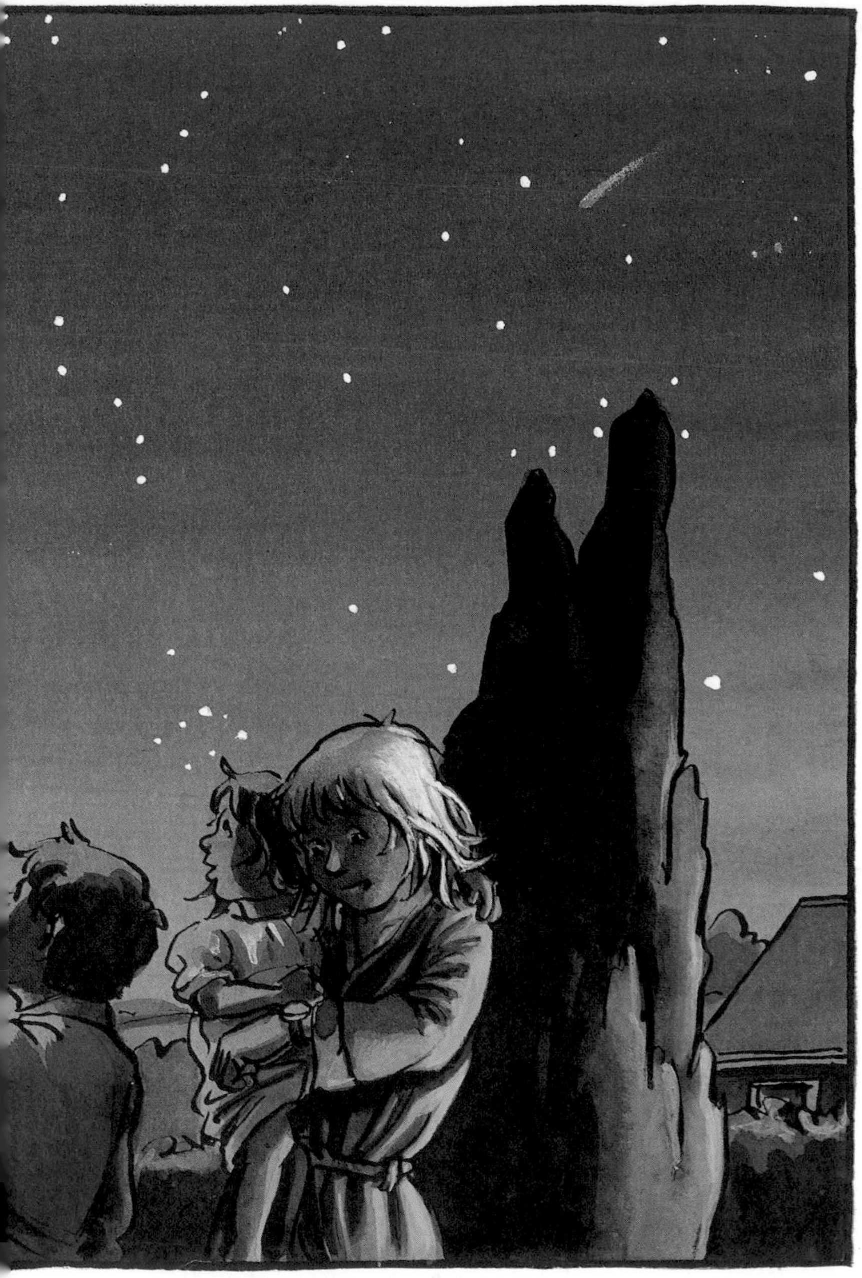

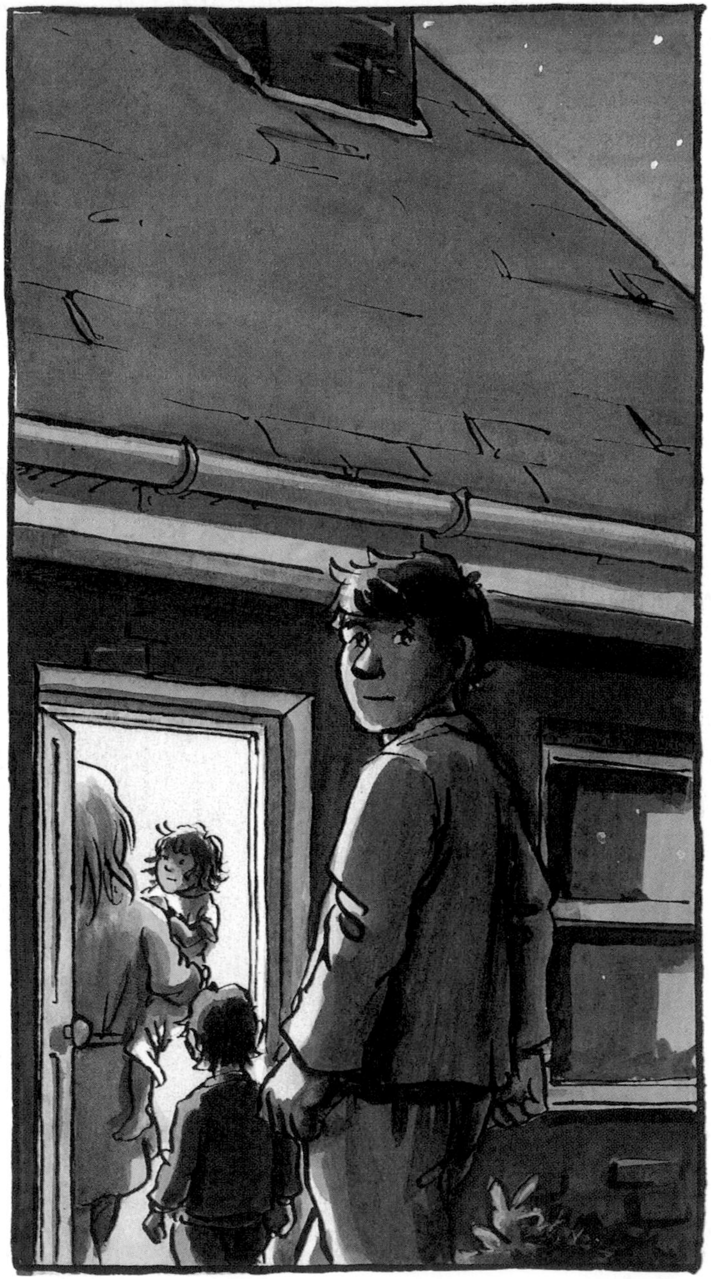

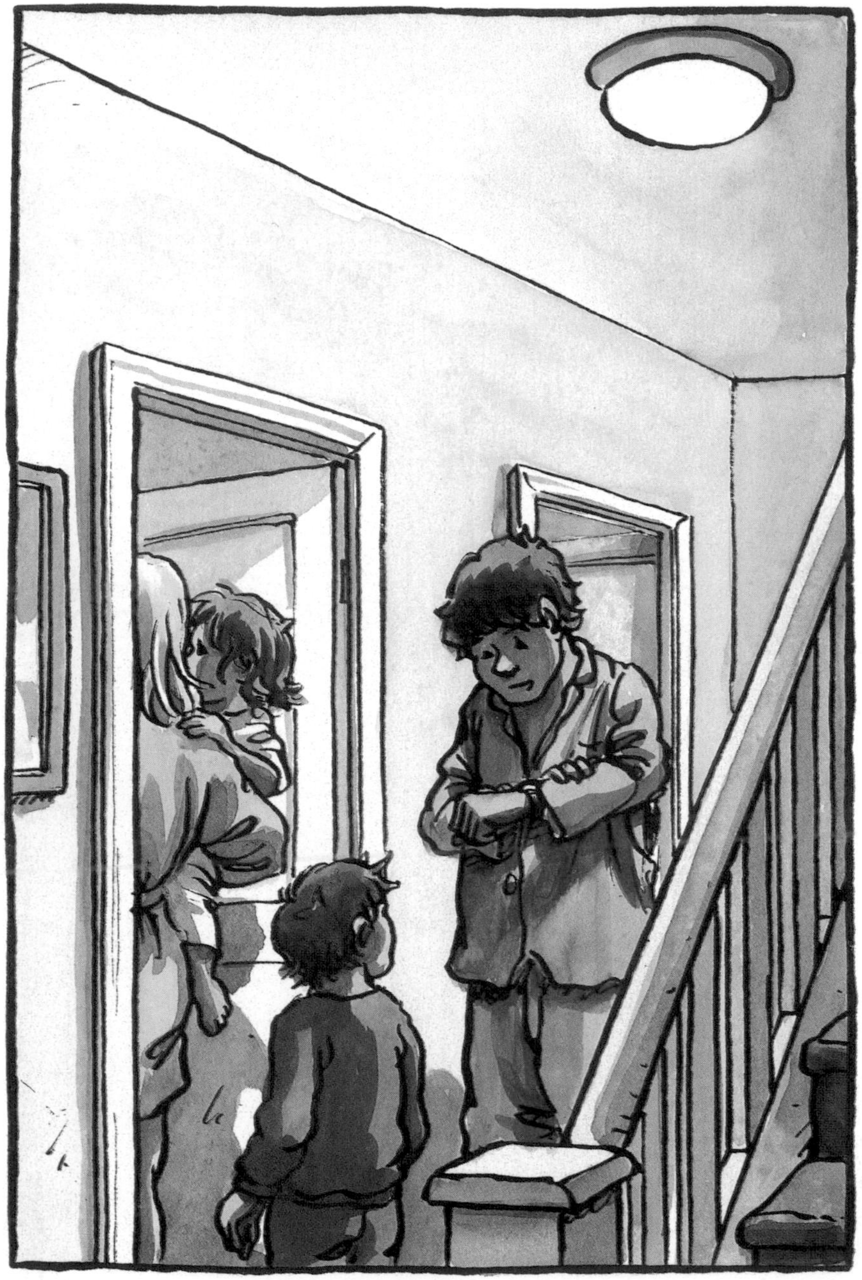
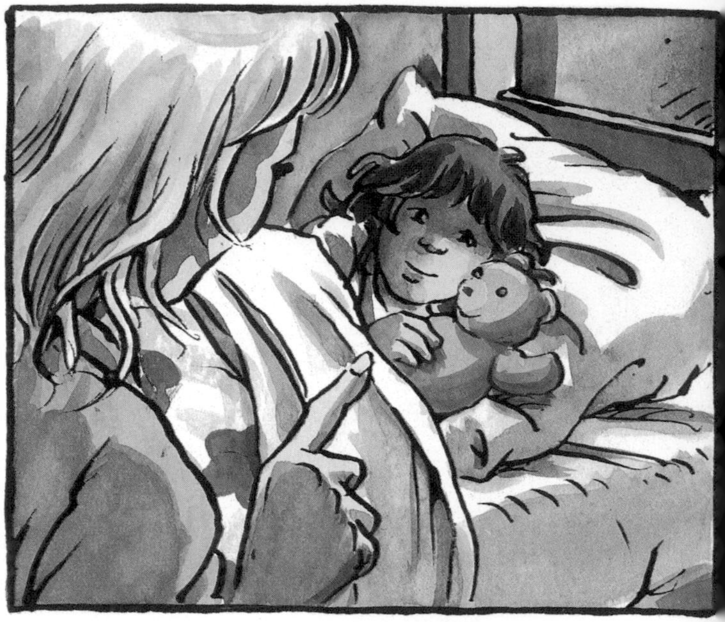
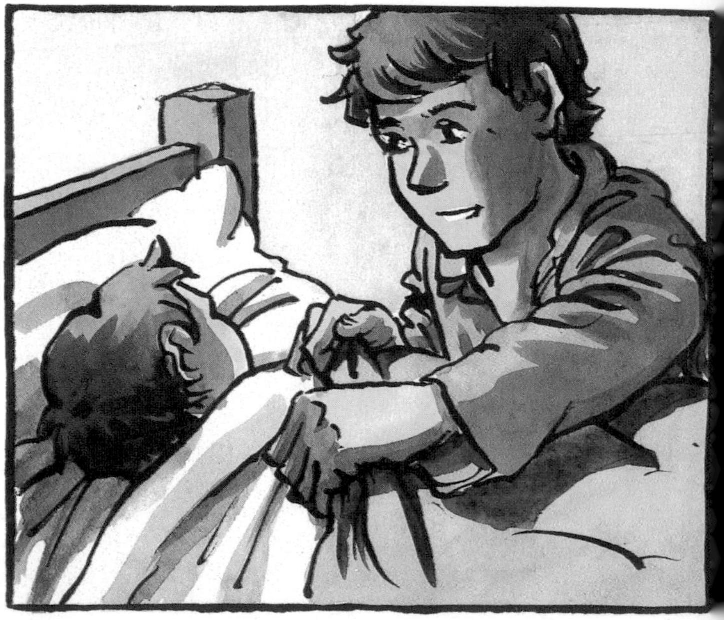

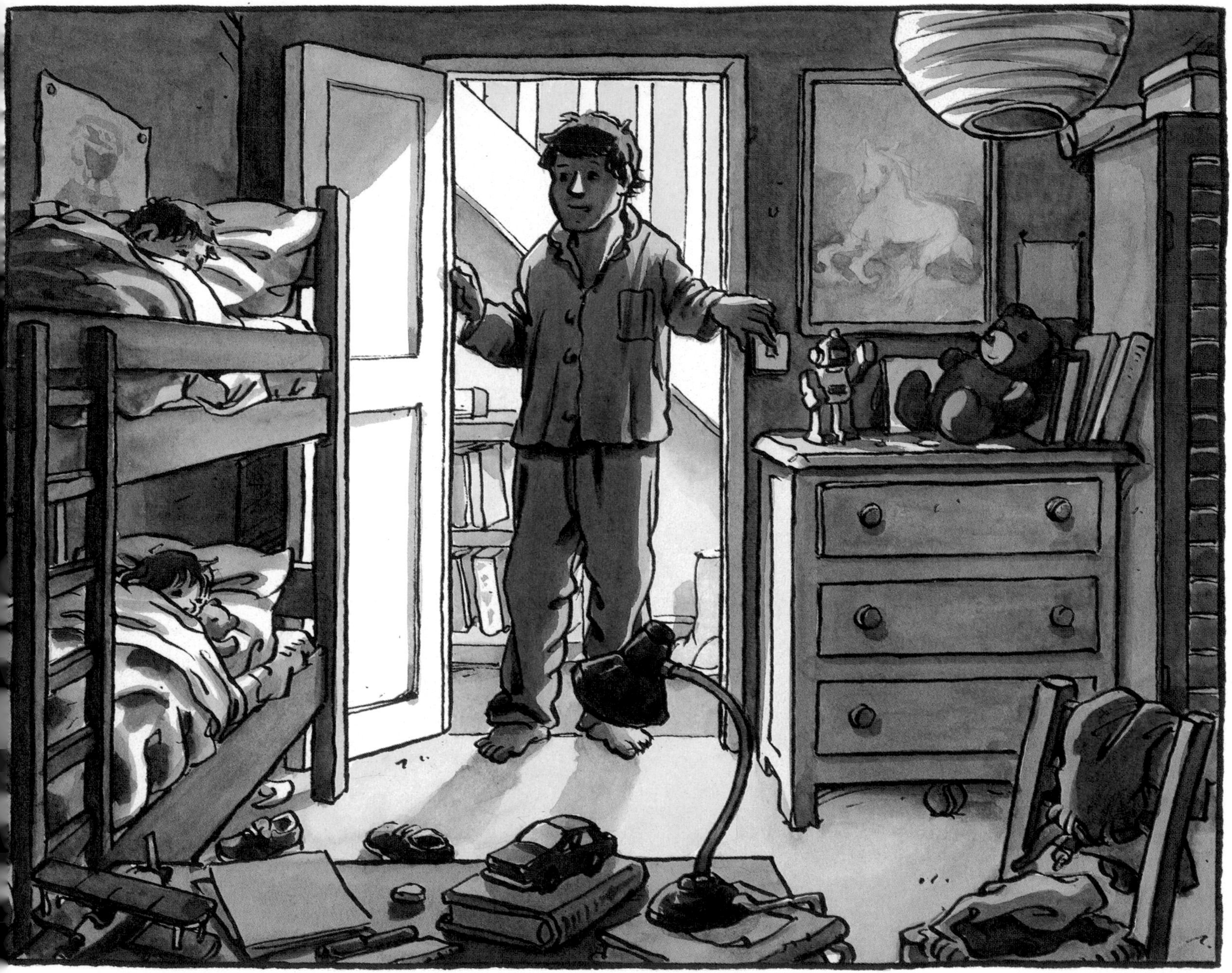

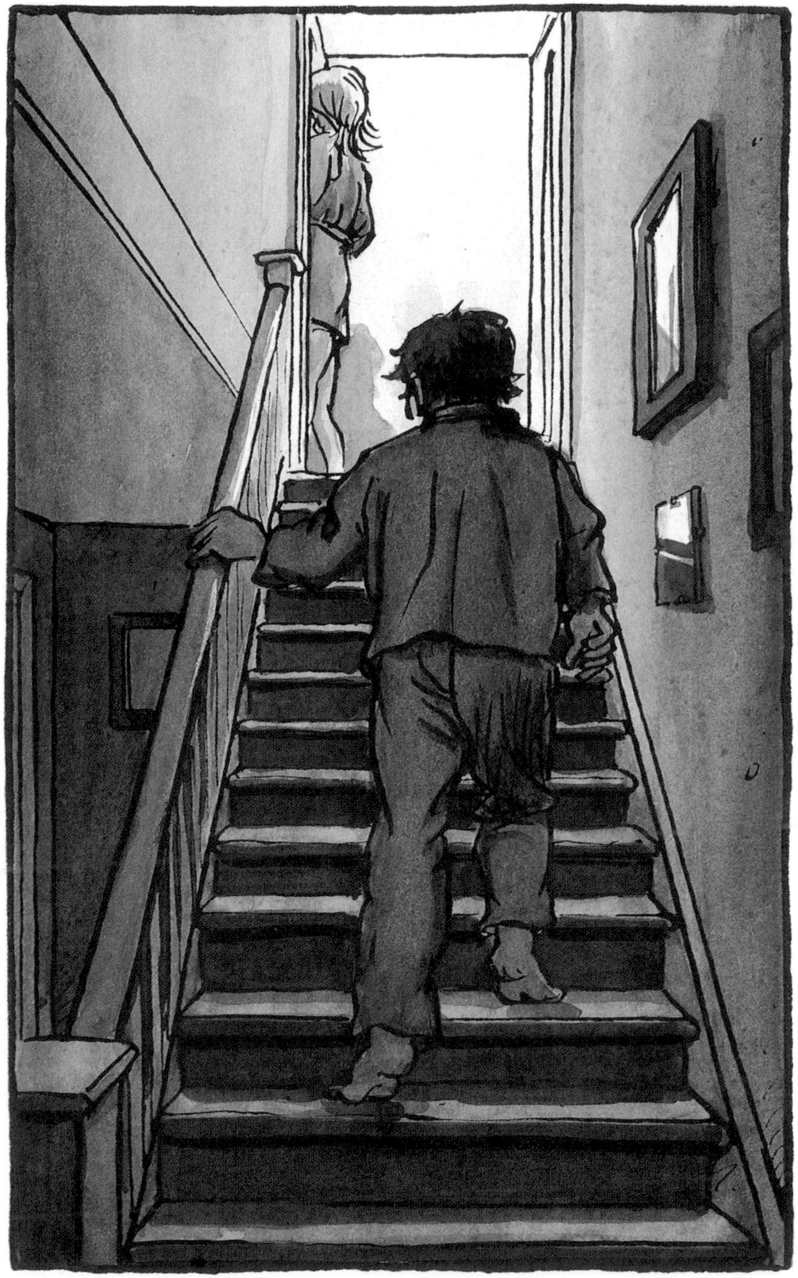
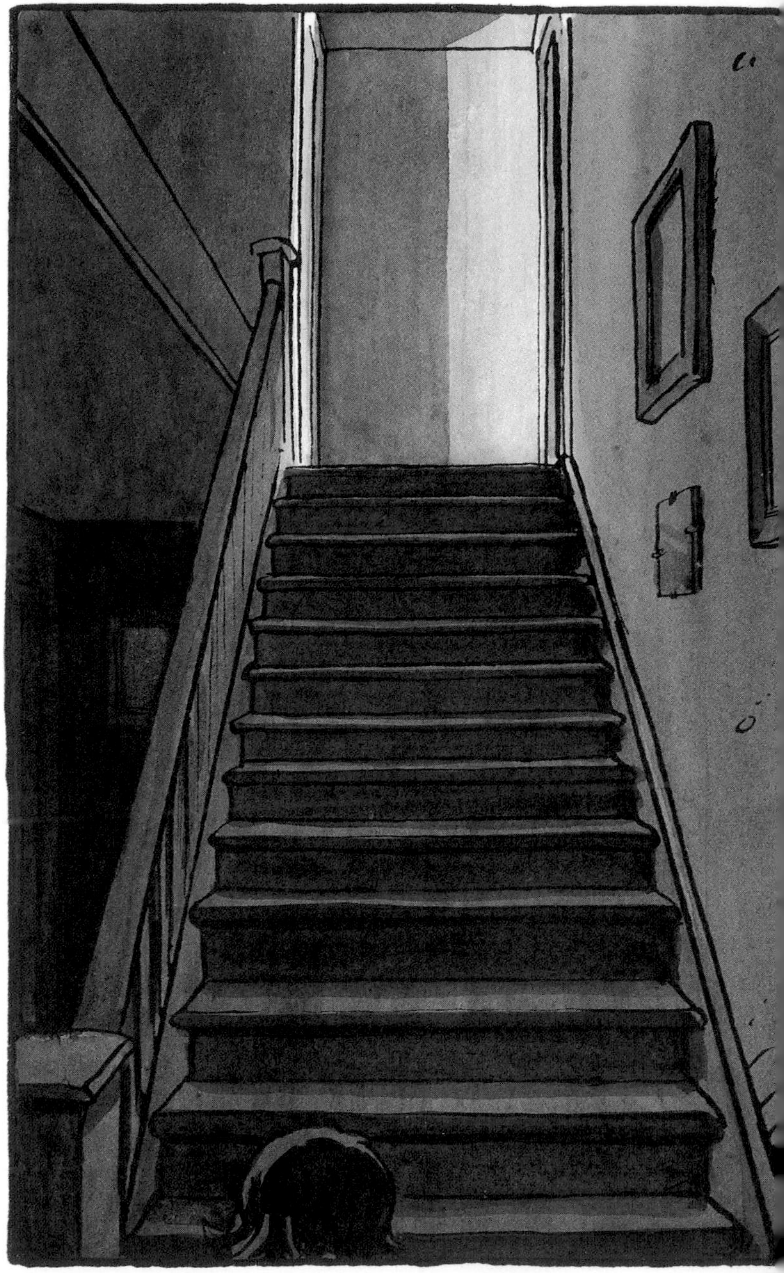

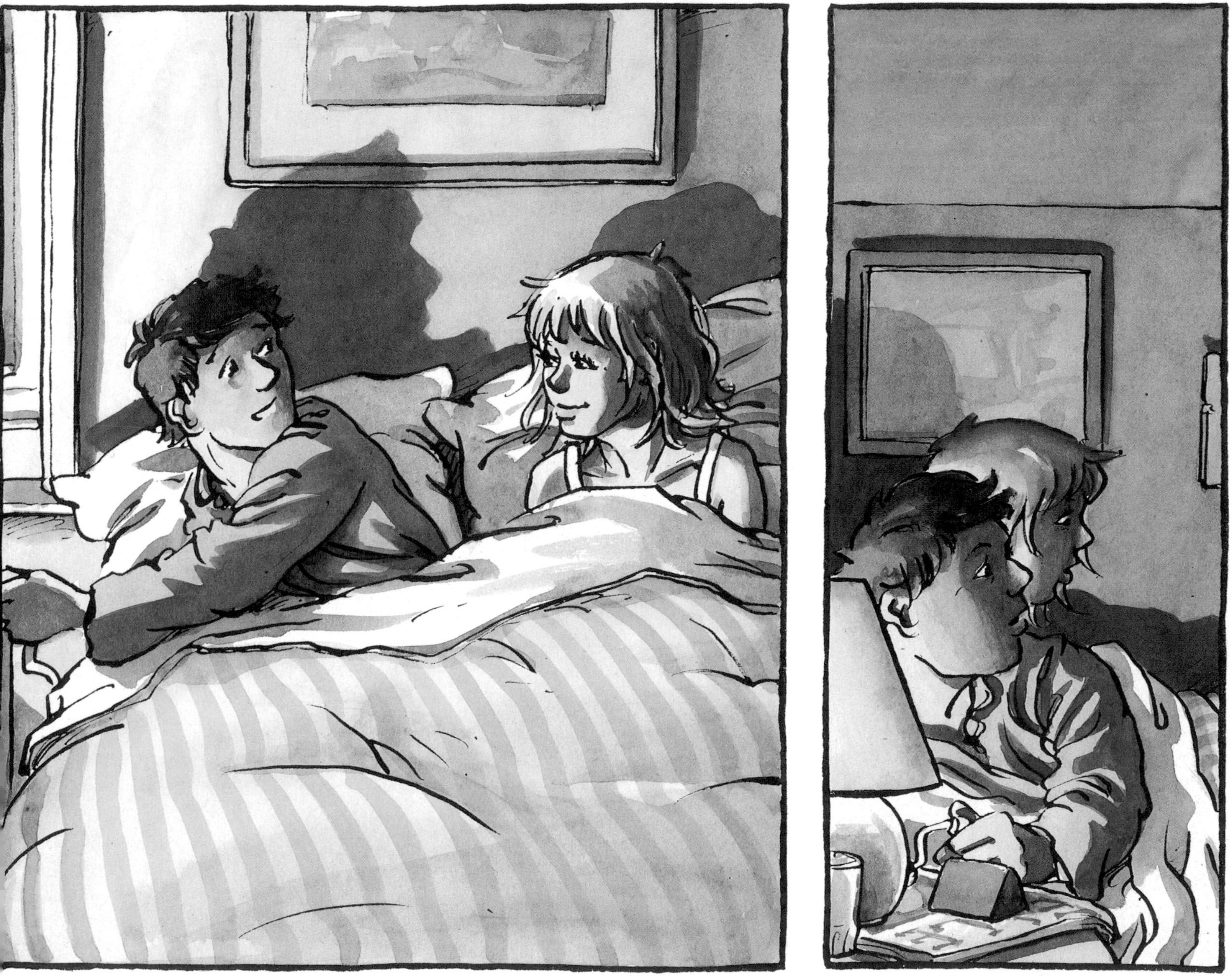

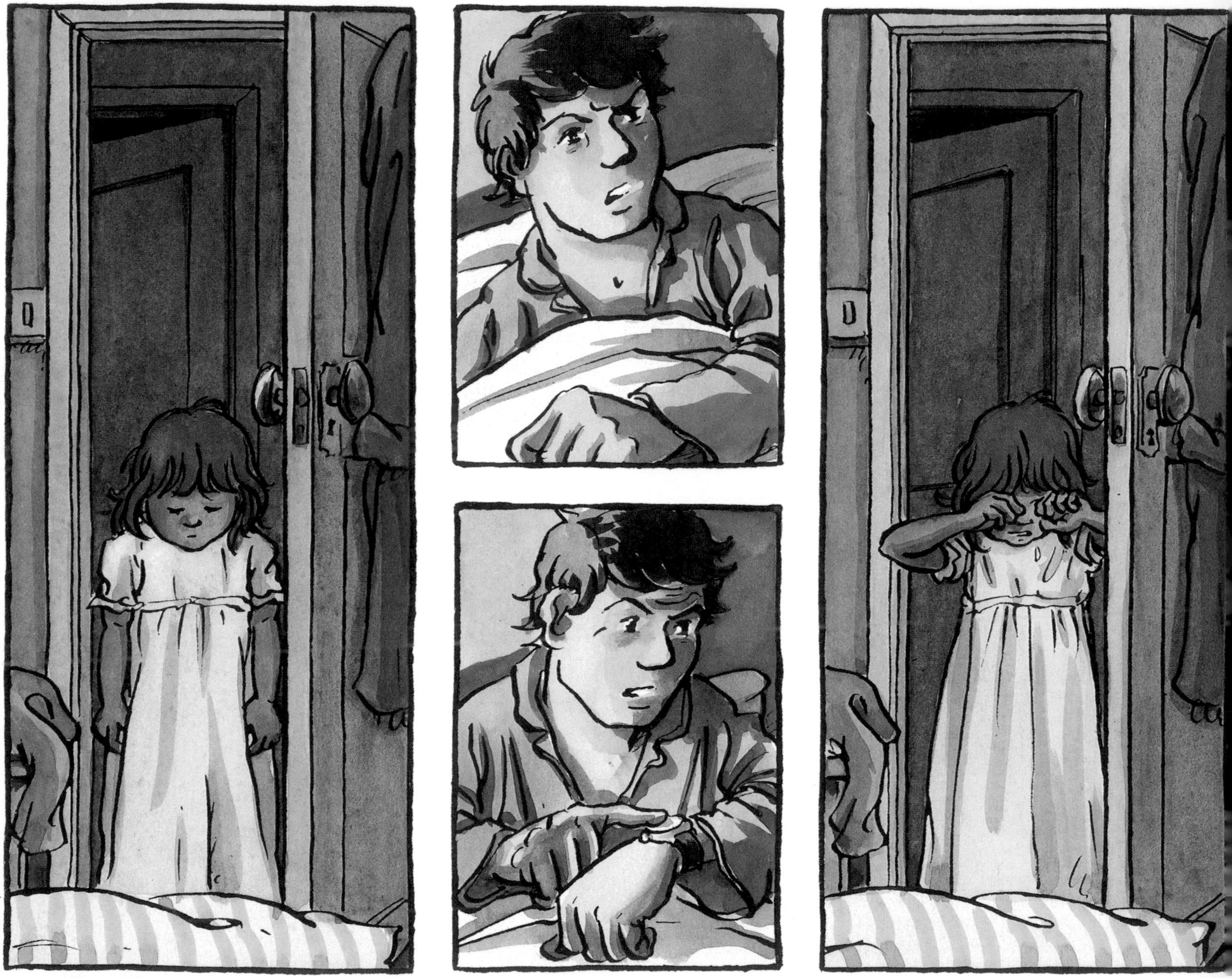

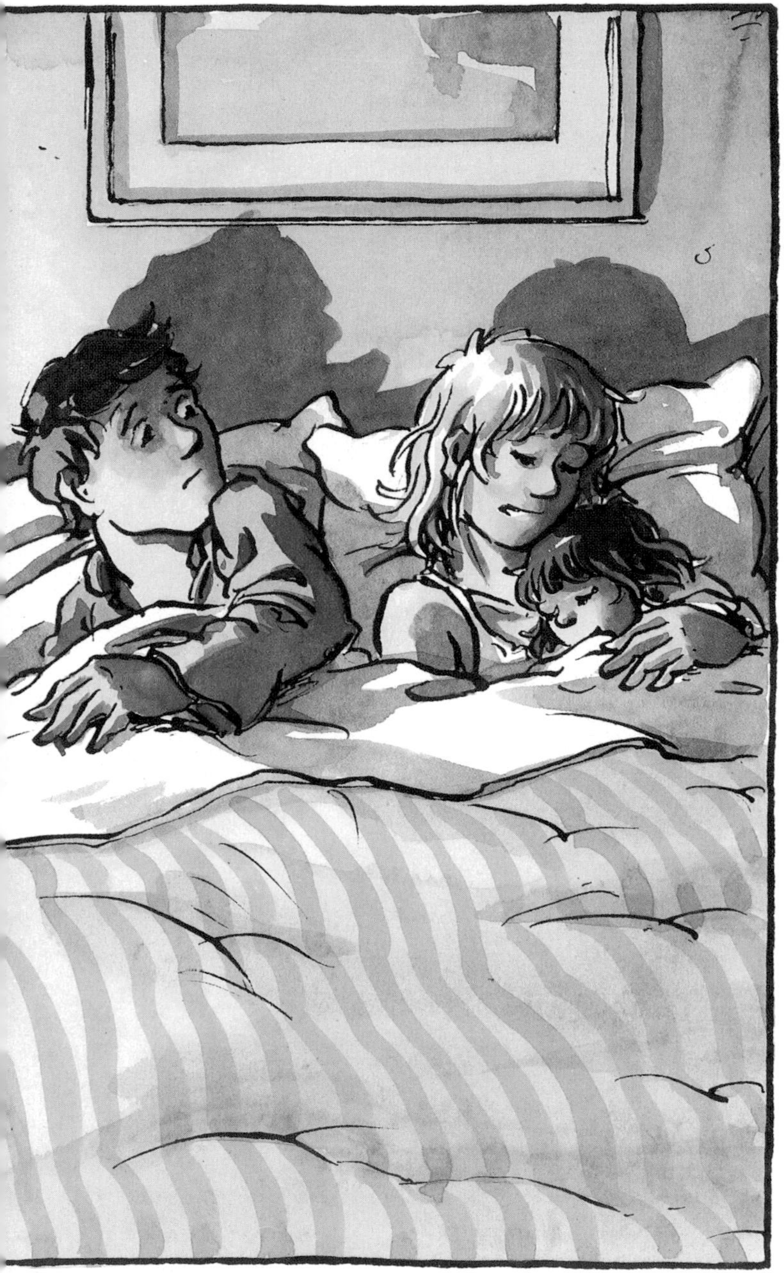
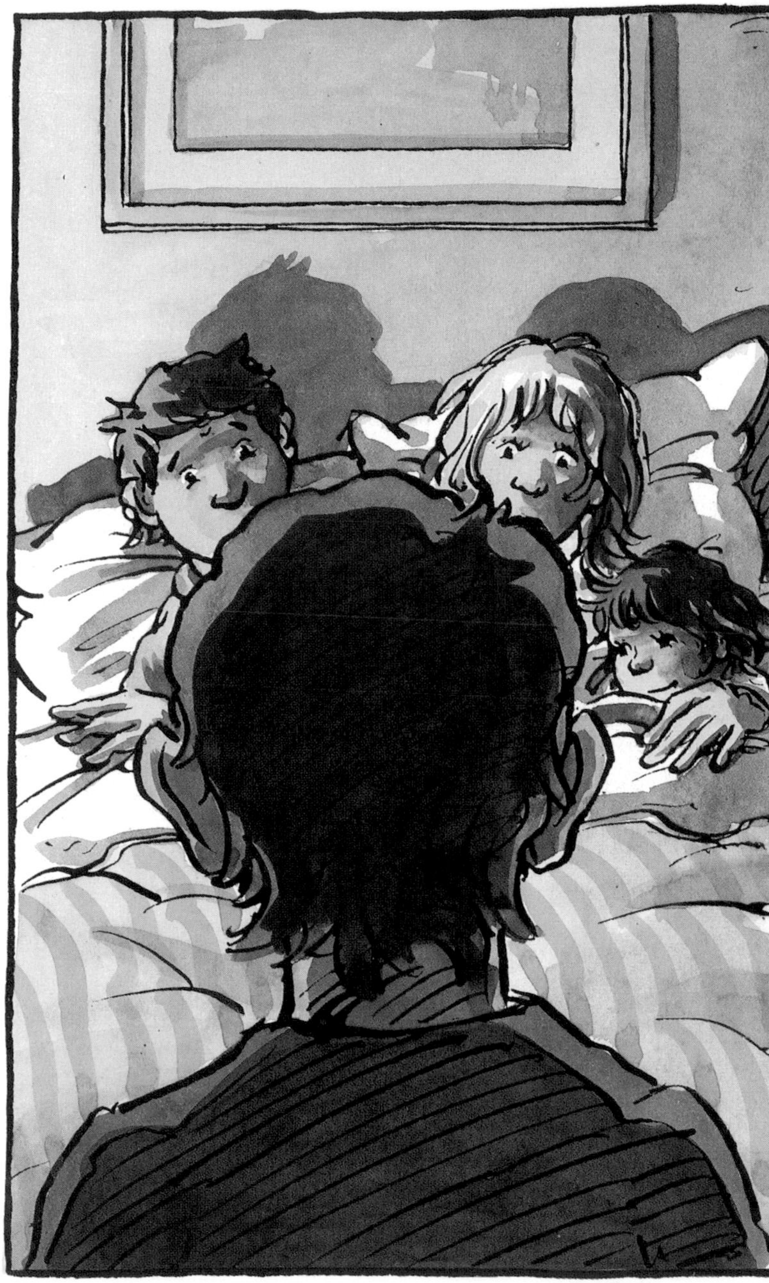

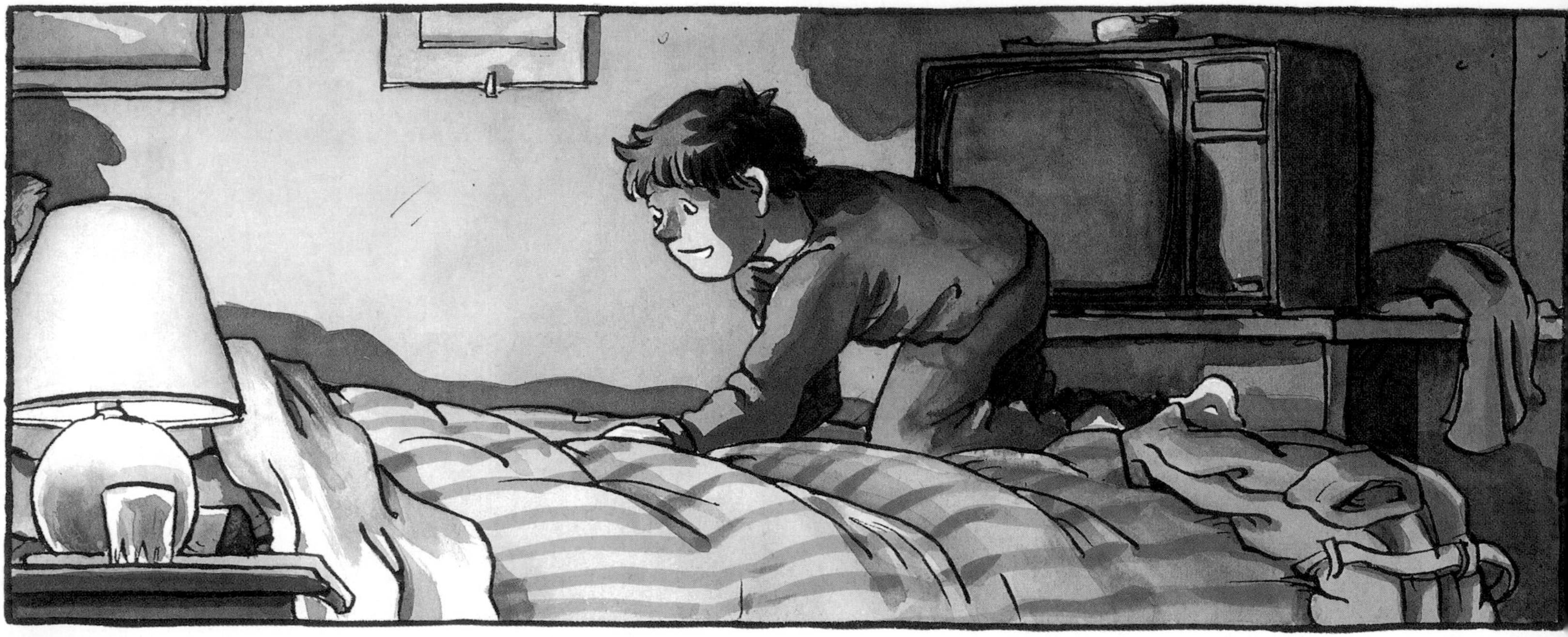
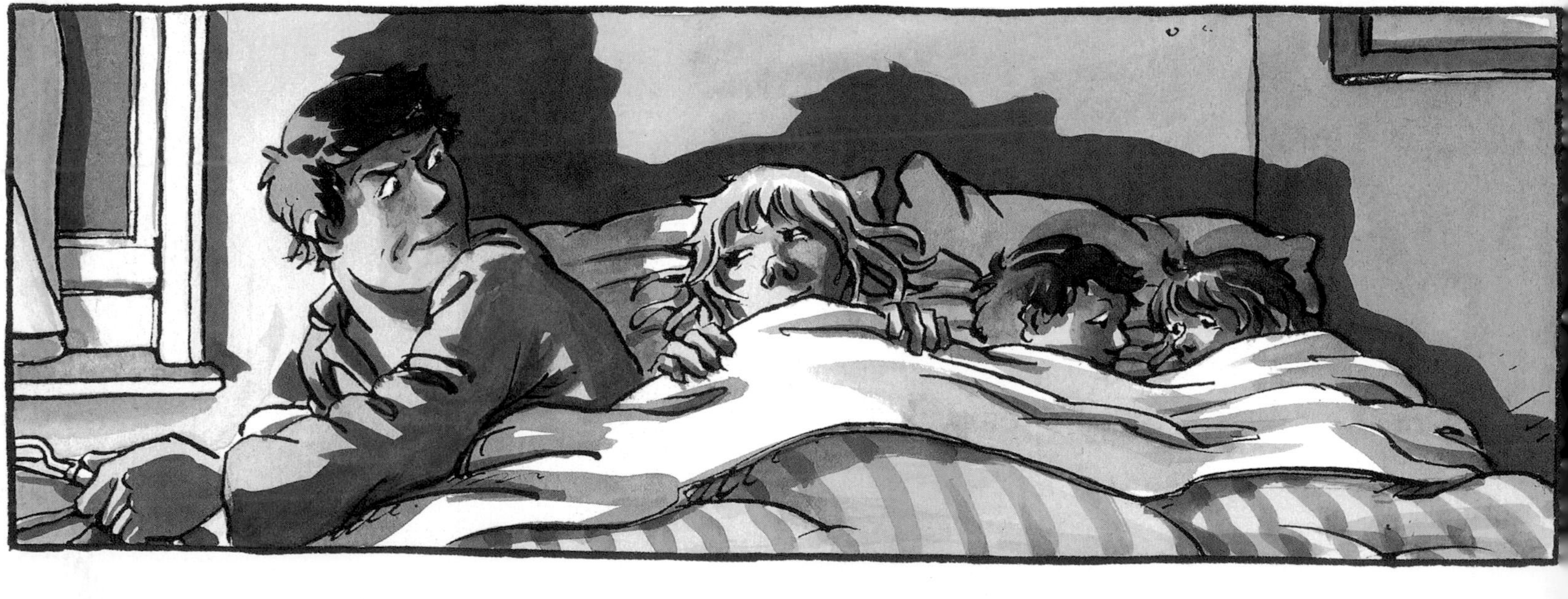

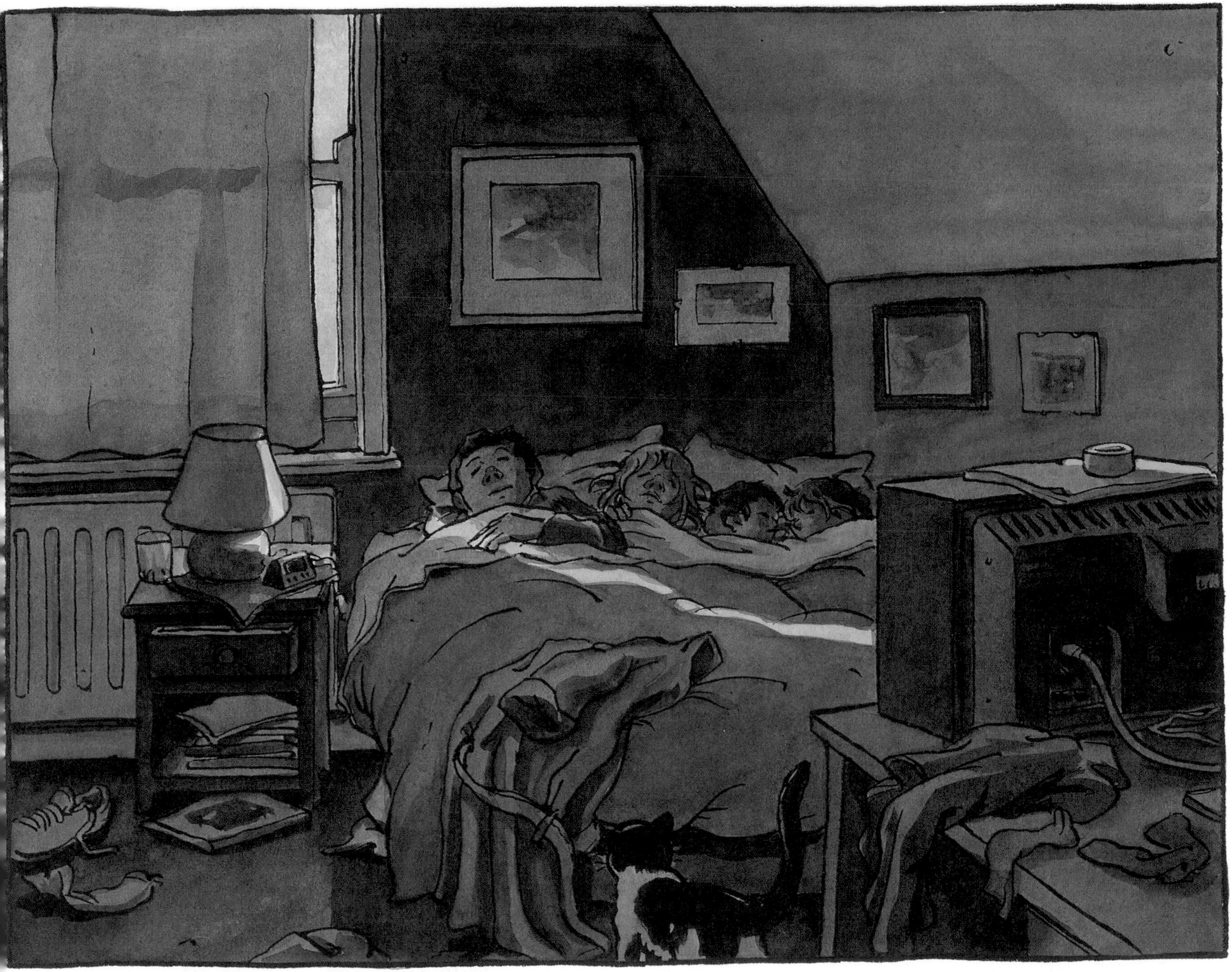

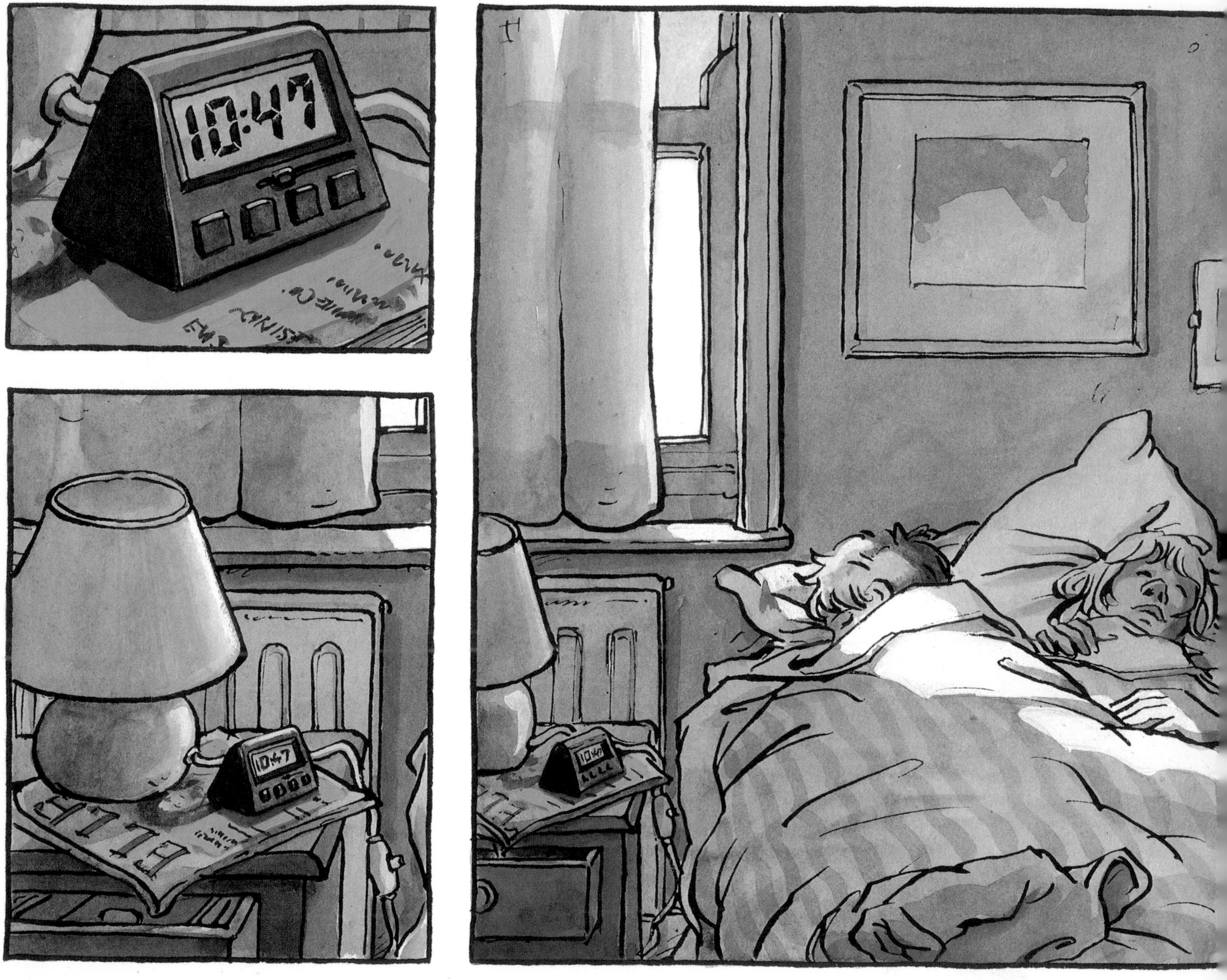
10:47

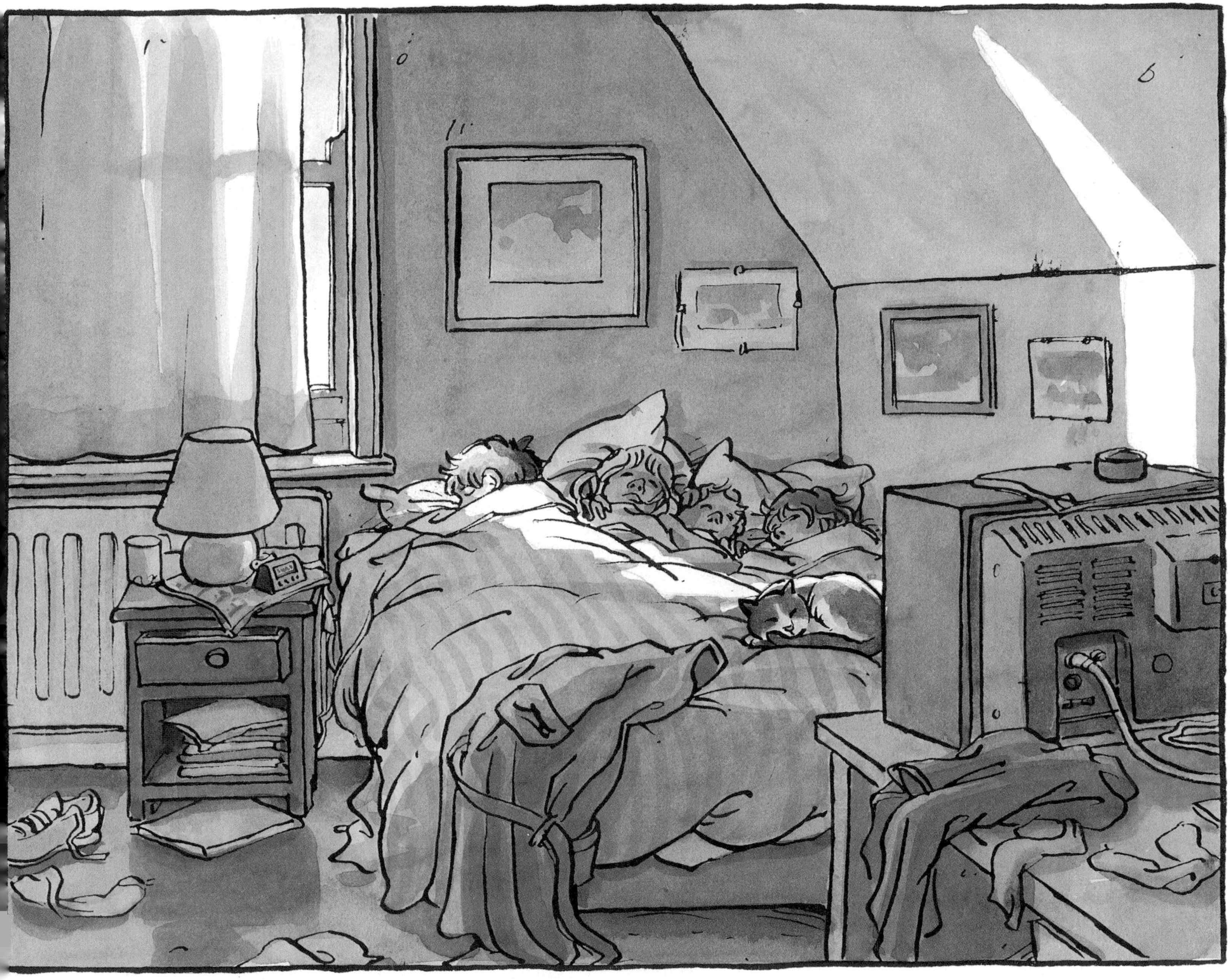

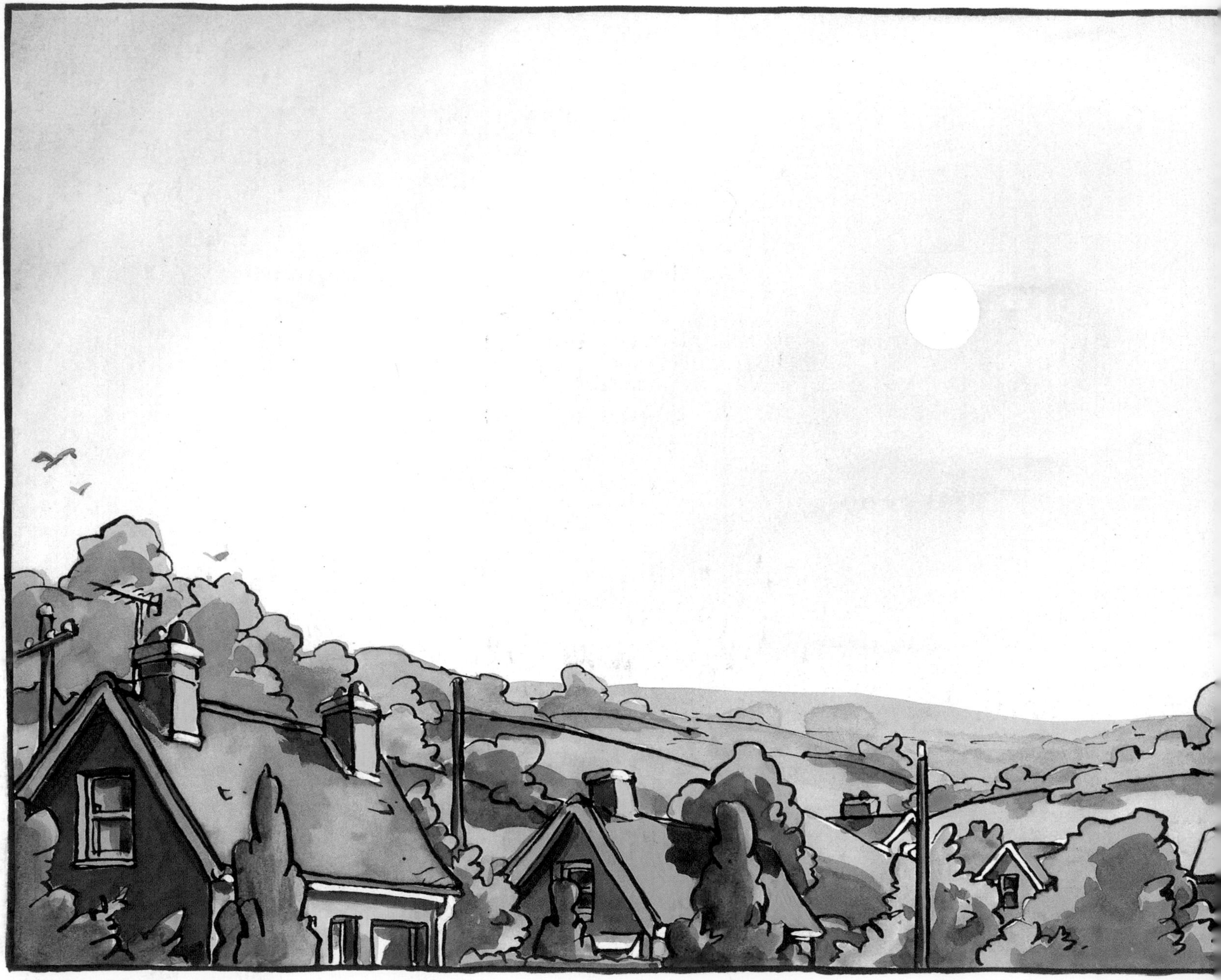